Say it was Murder

A McShan Thriller

Stephen Mertz

ROUGH
EDGES
PRESS

Praise for Say it was Murder

"Reminds me of Ross MacDonald's early (and best) Lew Archer novels!"
– Evan Lewis

"The characters are great, Southern Arizona is used to startlingly vivid effect, the dialogue snaps, crackles and pops, and the plot burns like a wildfire!"
– The Thrilling Detective Website

"Innovative . . . The Arizona setting is painted with stark colors to reveal a vibrant rural landscape and culture. The prose, smooth as glass, has the strength of an Arizona thunderstorm."
– Ben Boulden

Praise for Stephen Mertz

"Stephen Mertz writes a hard edged, fast paced thriller for those who like their tales straight and sharp!"
– Joe R. Lansdale

"One of my favorite writers...a born storyteller...Enjoy!"
– Max Allan Collins

"One of the best adventure writers of our time!"
– James Reasoner

"Stephen Mertz is a Grandmaster of action adventure novels!"
– MensAdventureMagazine&Books.com

"Stephen Mertz is the best action writer I've read in a long time!"
– Brent Towns

Rough Edges Press
An Imprint of Wolfpack Publishing
5130 S. Fort Apache Rd. 215-380
Las Vegas, NV 89148

roughedgespress.com

Paperback ISBN 978-1-68549-083-6
eBook ISBN 978-1-68549-082-9

For Paul Bishop

Say it was Murder

Chapter One

I sat behind the steering wheel of a van parked across and at the opposite end of the block from the house under surveillance: a four-story brownstone with a front porch overhang. Dark as every other house along the street except for a single light from a third-story window. A streetlight, suspended above the next intersection, barely offered enough wattage to reach the shadows of an alley that ran past the brownstone.

A crisp chill to the air. Traffic noise and city sounds at two A.M. were reduced to a background mumble. A dog was barking somewhere. Otherwise, the street slumbered. A student housing neighborhood adjacent to the University of Denver campus. School night. The tree-lined street also lined with the inky shapes of bumper-to-bumper parked vehicles, many of them of a vintage preceding this decade.

In the passenger seat next to me, Big Earl eyed the dashboard clock.

"No pedestrian traffic for the last fifteen minutes."

He was a mountain of a man. His attention shifted back to the world beyond the windshield. "No vehicular traffic in seven."

Danny's voice crackled as if inside my head. He and Samantha would be holding their position around the corner, thus bottling up both ends of the alley.

"We going in or what?"

Each of us was equipped with a personal communicator set consisting of a nearly invisible earpiece and a tiny microphone in the band of a wristwatch.

Samantha's voice said, clipped and dispassionate like always: *"Listen. There's a sweet kid up there in harm's way. I'm going in if no one else is."*

And that was Sam and Danny in a nutshell.

The four of us respected each other and were glad we'd been teamed up by the head office. That didn't mean we weren't a mixed bag of nuts. Determined individualists would be one way to put it.

We'd flown into Denver separately and rendezvoused at the local branch office of *Honeycutt Personal Services,* and everyone genuinely glad to reconnect. As a unit we'd been through situations together in the past; the sort of street stuff that bonds a unit when your survival depends on the ones covering your back. This breeds a level of trust that runs deeper than you'll find in many marriages. Ask any cop or soldier.

A muted beep filled the van's interior.

The craggy, hawk-faced visage of Agatha Honeycutt illuminated the small Skype screen mounted on the dash.

The image barked at me. *"McShan! I want a report!"*

You couldn't see the motorized wheelchair or her expansive girth that overflowed from it. Easy enough to visualize, though, as much a part of the woman as the rasping shrew voice. Miss Honeycutt is sixty-three years old and looks it. Heavyset. Freckled, jowly chocolate features. Salt and pepper hair worn in a dated bouffant. Irascible as hell. She'd inherited the agency after her father died three years ago. She turned the business around into a thriving enterprise, partnering up with people that included ex-law enforcement and ex-military. Honeycutt Personal Services now had offices in all fifty states and provided a wide range of services from computer security to kidnap protection.

I said, "What have you got, Agatha?"

"What the hell do you mean, what have I got? I've been waiting for the past hour for a goddamn report. Why haven't you checked in?"

In the bucket seat next to me, I sensed Big Earl tighten up. His black features were unreadable. Earl didn't much care for Miss Agatha, as we referred to her. None of us liked her. But the pay was good. She called us her street soldiers.

I told the face on the screen, "Now you know better than to put me on a job and then bird-dog my ass. I thought we had an understanding."

"Don't sass me, McShan. The girl. You're sure she's up there?"

I eyed the lighted window on the third floor of the brownstone.

"We think so."

"So contact the authorities."

"We don't have time."

"What do you mean, you don't have time?"

"Sam wants to move in now."

"You hush that fuss. You're the point man. Earl, are you there?"

Big Earl leaned into range of the screen. "I'm here."

"I know you and Samantha have a history, Big Earl. Don't you let her take over on this. She's a hot head. You boys follow my orders, hear? Get the police in there. I don't want the agency involved in a shooting scrape."

Earl said, "Sam's right. We can't trust these punks what have the girl. We've got to close in."

A derisive snort of displeasure from the screen.

Agatha said to me, *"You found the girl. That was the mission. That's the end of it. Do as you're told, McShan. Contact the authorities."*

This case had been a bear from the beginning.

Poppy Kincaid was a bright, attractive but withdrawn, chubby fifteen-year-old. The daughter of a San Francisco real estate tycoon and his class-obsessed wife. The girl had disappeared without a trace from an exclusive boarding school. The Honeycutt Agency was retained to track her down.

Interviews with classmates and faculty at the school. Reading between the lines with the parents. And from this emerged the portrait of a highly intelligent but troubled girl who belonged to a small clique of goth misfits at school. Her boyfriend played in a garage band until his death from a heroin overdose the month before. A few days before Poppy's disappearance, another of her goth friends slashed her wrists and bled to death in the early AM hours in the shower room of the women's dorm.

* * *

Poppy had hooked up with a trendy New Age cult and became a follower of a charismatic matriarchal leader who espoused a variety of eccentric notions —make that cons—from the channeling of dead spirits to cosmology to the notion that mankind was an experiment undertaken by extraterrestrials. The cult's front office had disavowed any knowledge of the girl's whereabouts, but I had gone with a hunch. Poppy was a minor and the cult was playing with dynamite. It was only after dire legal threats to shut down their entire operation that the Denver chapter leader agreed to cooperate.

A pair of the cult followers who had been assigned to "deliver" the girl turned out to be bad apples.

The third-floor light in the brownstone went out.

Danny's voice carried across the tac net.

"So are we waiting or what?"

Samantha: *"How do we know what's going on in that apartment? We're going in!"*

I said to the Skype face, "We can't wait."

Agatha said, *"Damn you, McShan, don't you dare hang up on me. You follow orders or I'll—"*

I disconnected. The screen went dark.

I said, "Let's do it, people."

Big Earl and I exited the van, easing the doors shut soundlessly. We filled our hands with hardware from concealed holsters. We each packed a 9mm Glock 17. We jogged across the street, footfalls echoing off the pavement. We gained a position to either side of the brownstone's front entrance.

I reached down and tried the door handle, knowing it would be locked. It was. I glanced at Earl. He was the sort who had memorized every step of every procedure in the book. He positioned himself behind me, slightly to my side to avoid a line of possible fire from inside the house, pistol held in a two-handed stance to provide me with cover. I lifted my right foot and launched a kick at the door's lock.

The door busted in off its hinges.

We stormed inside, falling away to either side of the door. A well-lighted, tiled foyer. Rows of mailboxes to the left. A hallway dead ahead. A stairway leading up.

Danny and Samantha could be heard gaining forcible entry through the alley entrance.

Then a clatter of footfalls descending the staircase. Practically tumbling into view, because they were in such a hurry: two shabby guys in their teens—jeans, sneakers, T-shirts, toting handguns—dragging along Poppy Kincaid behind them.

The girl was disheveled. Vacant eyes, numbed by fear or whatever they'd pumped into her.

I caught the first one across the mouth with a swipe of my pistol, breaking bone, splattering droplets of blood. He bounced back against the wall, and pitched face forward down the steps to the floor.

Big Earl was waiting. He kicked the gun out of the kid's hand. He snapped the boy's arm to the small of the back and kneed him hard there, handcuffing him.

I tracked my weapon on the one holding onto the girl. His free hand was filled with a heavy piece. A .44 Magnum.

I said, "Drop it! *Now!*"

Big Earl drew a bead on the kid too.

Earl added, "And step away from the girl."

The kid hesitated. Wild, jacked up eyes. A razor's-edge, anything-can-happen tick of time. Beads of sweat like tiny pearls along his mussed hairline. But he didn't drop the gun.

I said, "Let it go, son. I'm no cowboy. I don't want to shoot anybody. Lose it."

He licked his lips. Wired eyes flared. He didn't say a thing. He started tracking the gun in my direction.

I shot him once in the upper thigh.

The gunshot was louder than hell.

He shrieked. His gun clattered onto the wooden stairs, but I barely heard it because my ears were ringing. His knees buckled. He released his hold on Poppy Kincaid. He tumbled, landing next to his partner on the tiled floor at Big Earl's feet.

Then Danny and Samantha appeared from around the corner of the hallway. That's how fast it went down.

Sam holstered her pistol and went straight to Poppy, embracing the girl like a big sister, shielding the girl's traumatized eyes, guiding her down the steps and out to the front porch.

The apartment building was coming to life around us. Sleepy, tentative voices calling to each other, wondering what was going on.

Earl handcuffed the wounded one, who was whining mightily. Earl reached for his cell phone, assuring him that an ambulance was on the way.

Earl added, "Let's hope for your sake, dummy, that the ambulance gets here faster than police backup."

Earl was speaking to the 911 operator.

Danny said to me, "Nice shooting."

I barely heard them. The ringing in my ears

sounded like a dozen church bells. We should have worn ear plugs.

Then the place was filling with cops.

The cavalry—in this case an over-amped SWAT team—had arrived.

Chapter Two

The next day . . .

S he was barefoot. She wore a western cut blue blouse and pressed blue jeans. In the morning sunshine, standing there in the doorway of her Indian tipi, she looked terrific.

Yes, tipi.

Not a real one. Hers was one of six identical cone-shaped structures that had been designed and constructed to look from a distance like tipis. They were on Highway 80 a few miles south of Bisbee where the state road makes its flatland run for the Mexican border. It's the primary, well-traveled route north across Cochise County from Agua Prieta, Sonora to Interstate 10, sixty miles north, and the rest of the world.

The tipis showed their age in the daylight but would no doubt look, when viewed with the proper perspective, like romantic little bungalows under an Arizona moon. That had to have been the intent back in the day when such places were called motor courts.

Highway 80 had been well-traveled long before the Interstate. These days the owners, whoever they might be, were doing their best to keep up appearances. A recent coat of white paint partially disguised minor structural damage visible at the peak of each "tipi" where decades of hot summers, cold winters and heavy monsoonal rains had done their work.

The presence of a vehicle in each parking space of the neighboring units suggested that the nostalgic aspect of *The Tipi Lodge* still appealed to tourists and lovebirds with a taste for the rustic. Beyond the tipis was a convenience store with gas pumps and a doublewide residential trailer, most likely home of the owner or manager.

I braked the rental Jeep Wrangler next to a four-year-old red Mazda parked beside Unit #4, the address I'd been provided with. My new client had come to the door of her tipi to greet me.

She was a small-boned blonde. Nicely shaped. Forty, or thereabouts. Smile lines around intelligent green eyes did not distract from the beauty of high cheekbones and a strong jaw line.

She said, "Hello, there."

She held a small black mutt of a dog that struggled happily to escape her arms. She set the dog down. The little guy scampered over to greet me, making quite a production of smelling both shoes and both cuffs before dashing back and forth between us. The woman left the doorway, extending a hand.

"Thank you for coming. I'm Marna Richards." Her handshake was the kind a man likes from a woman, firm and confident, not indifferent and not overly forceful to impress. She knelt and extended her arms to the cute mutt. "Come on, Beauregard."

The scruffy black blur leapt into her arms with an ear-to-ear doggie smile, his stubby tail wagging madly. My new client cooed in its ear. Beauregard relaxed contentedly in the cradle of her arms.

My client looked at the panoramic scenery of desert, mountains, and sky. She drew in a deep breath and exhaled with enthusiasm.

"Isn't it a perfectly beautiful day?"

I winced against the brassy sun. It was the middle of August and hot.

"Nice enough. Another scorcher unless we get rain."

It was the monsoon season in this high desert land. It would often rain in the late afternoons, but not every day. When it didn't rain, it just got muggy.

It was the midday after the windup of the Denver job. I'd dismissed the team. Agatha Honeycutt had wasted no time handing me my next assignment. She liked to keep her foot soldiers busy.

I'd called her, delivered my report that I knew was being recorded and would be transcribed for the clients, and navigated the usual barbs and cussing about my "cowboy ways," by which Miss Agatha meant my inability to obey the rules and take orders. That same complaint had dogged me throughout military service, a fitful career in law enforcement, not to mention my illustrious high school football career and a few bad marriages.

I, in turn as always, reminded Agatha that she tolerates me because I get results that earn her agency huge retainers no matter how many rules I break.

With that out of the way, I was informed that Marna Richards had retained the agency. I was the operative being dispatched. Agatha called it "a misbehaving daughter job."

I'd caught some snooze time on the red-eye flight from Denver to Tucson, followed by a few more hours of snooze time after my predawn check-in to Bisbee's historic Copper Queen Hotel. The accommodations were comfortable enough. A bit over the top in its faux 1880's mining boom motif, but the staff was nice.

Bisbee is a picturesque mountain town located in the extreme southeastern corner of Arizona. Its century-long reign as a top copper producer waned with the shutdown of the enormous Phelps-Dodge pit mine forty years ago. The population of Bisbee rapidly dwindled to its current five-thousand-plus inhabitants, some of whom are retirees and business owners while the majority can only be described as neo-hippies. It's a vibrant, artistic bohemian paradise for the dropout set.

Marna Richards thoroughly sized me up during our opening exchange of pleasantries, from my boots to my jeans to my black T-shirt to my hair that was a mite too shaggy for current fashion.

She said, "I hope you don't mind me saying this but, well, you don't look like a private detective."

I nodded at the Jeep.

"I left my fedora and trench coat in the vehicle. Didn't think I'd need them this early in the day."

A single, muted *ping!* emanated from a pocket of her jeans.

She set the dog down. Beauregard accepted this with good humor. Marna produced a cell phone from her pocket and glanced at the screen.

Ever the gentleman, I said, "I'll step aside while you take your call," and started to move beyond earshot.

She pocketed the phone. "No, don't. That's all right. It's not a call. Come on in."

Beauregard trailed her inside. I trailed Beauregard.

Inside, she snagged a pack of cigarettes from a counter near the door. She shook loose a cigarette. Got it going with a Bic lighter. She regarded the cigarette with a frown.

"I'm trying to quit. I made a resolution last New Year's Eve. One cigarette every hour on the hour. That may sound like a lot but, see, I understand that breaking a habit like mine takes time. I was a two-pack-a-day girl."

I said, "And the year's more than half over. I'm impressed."

I was, too.

She said, "Next year I'm going to give up smoking altogether." She spoke through a cloud of exhaled grey smoke. "I'm the persistent type once I commit. I've got a stick-to-it nature. You watch. This time next year, I'll be smoke free."

She reached over to close the door after us.

I nodded to an oversized pair of brogans on the outside stoop. They looked brand new.

"Those have to belong to a mighty big boy."

Rule number one: Be aware of your surroundings. I needed to know if I should be expecting company during our interview.

Marna Richards grinned.

"There's no big boy. Those are to make any stranger knocking at my door *think* there's a big old man living here with me, protecting me."

"Clever," I said, and meant it.

The interior of the tipi could be considered cozy or cramped. Imitation pine paneling. Mismatched furnishings consisting of a double bed, dresser, straight-backed chair at a small writing table and a wall-mounted TV. An open door led to the bathroom. Beauregard scampered around our ankles in a tizzy over new human energy (i.e., me) intruding in their space.

Marna sat on the edge of the bed. She gestured to the chair for me to have a seat, her every gesture leaving a gray trail of cigarette smoke. Two open suitcases were spread across the bed and a stuffed backpack rested on the table. She patted her lap with her free hand. That was all Beauregard needed for another short leap that reclaimed his lapdog status, forgetting all about me. Marna stroked behind the mutt's ear, using her index finger. The little guy closed his eyes and zoned out. Who wouldn't?

She said, "Beauregard and I only met three weeks ago, believe it or not. He came up to me when I was doing my laundry in Chattanooga. I asked around but everyone I talked to said he was a neighborhood stray. So we did us some traveling, didn't we, Beau?" The dog's raggedy tail gave a single slight twitch at the sound of his name. Marna said, "My mom passed away two months ago."

"I'm sorry."

"It's okay. She was in terrible pain. It was a blessed release. That's her, over there." She gestured to a framed photo on the counter. A studio shot. Marna's mother was an older, heavier Marna. "I'm from Minnesota," Marna said. "That's where Dad was from. But my mom was born and raised in the Deep South.

Charleston. She missed it something terrible. We must've watched *Gone with the Wind* together at least twenty times when I was growing up. So after she . . . after she left us, I decided to take her ashes on a personal tour of the South. I spread her ashes in special places all over down there. Civil War battlegrounds. Places that were mentioned in *Gone with the Wind*. The whole bit. It was a long trip and I just got in early this morning. Did it all by my lonesome. I'd get scared to death passing those big eighteen wheelers on the interstate."

I let her chatter on like that for a couple of reasons.

I couldn't tell yet if any of this personal biography would have a direct bearing on why I was here. But then everything connects eventually and, in the meantime, it was bringing me up to speed on who I was dealing with. My professional eye detected no artifice. No phoniness. Eccentric, intelligent, pretty. That was my new client.

She'd smoked her cigarette straight down to the filter, taking care not to burn her fingertips as if smoking a joint. She extinguished it in a tin ashtray. She withdrew her cell phone, checked the time, sighed, and replaced the phone in her pocket.

She asked, "What sign are you?"

I said, "Aw, c'mon."

"No, really. I'm a Pisces. I have a reason for asking. It will tell me something I need to know."

"I'm a Taurus. We're not into astrology."

"Ha ha. Whatever. Taurus is good. Plodding. Durable. Goal oriented. Dependable."

"That's me, all right."

"Stodgy."

"Whoa. That's not me. I'm not stodgy."

She gazed longingly at her pack of cigarettes, only an arm's length away.

She said, "Damn, I could sure use a smoke." A deep breath followed by a fast, let's-get-down-to-business exhalation. Then she said, "Okay, let me tell you about why you're here."

Chapter Three

"My daughter's name is Janine. She's nineteen years old. Here's a picture of her."

She extended her smart phone so I could take a look. A similarity of facial resemblance ran through the three generations: the woman in the framed portrait on the counter, the woman seated before me, and the young woman in the smart phone screen. They all had high cheekbones, penetrating eyes and a strong jaw line. The main difference between the three was in the generational fullness of their features and hairstyles. As for personality, it's not always easy to discern character in a flat picture. They did share the same smile and the same eyes.

"Janine has become involved in some sort of New Age cult. A few miles from here, in fact. She grew up here in Cochise County. Her father, my ex-husband, still owns acreage just up the road. That's why I requested that the Honeycutt Agency send someone here to meet me. My daughter is of legal age, if only by a few months. I'm certainly aware of that. But she's young, and I'm her mother. I'm all in favor of marching to one's own drummer and seeking spiritual truth and all that. But I just don't think joining a cult is such a good idea."

I said, "What do you want me to do about it?"

Her eyes shadowed thoughtfully.

"Well, I guess I just want you to, um, nose around. I want you to check in on her day-to-day life. You know, investigate. Do whatever private detectives do. Find out what my daughter's up to with this group. If it's all of Janine's own free will and no harm is being done, well, at least then I'll know that and maybe I won't worry so much. But this close to the border . . . there's girls like Janine disappearing and being sold into sexual slavery. There's drugs. If my baby's in any sort of danger, I have a small inheritance and I'm willing to spend it on seeing that things are set right. Do you understand?"

"As you say, the girl is of legal age. How would you characterize your relationship with your daughter?"

The scraggly black bundle of fur in her lap rolled onto his back for a tummy scratch. Marna obliged. Her brow furrowed.

"It's not easy for a mother and daughter to get along when they're both headstrong and bullheaded free spirits. Janine has always been her daddy's little darling." Her good nature faltered for a heartbeat. A touch of resentment. She blinked once and it passed. She said, "Neither Janine or her father made it to my mother's memorial service. It wasn't easy for Janine. She had a choice to make. Her father is a successful businessman. He represents stability to a growing child. I don't. After our divorce, I became sort of a gypsy."

"When's the last time you spoke with Janine?"

"The day after her grandma died. She didn't act sad at all. Said she'd be in touch. That's when she told me about the cult. I researched them online. It's some guy who calls himself Birch Sunday. I ask you, what kind of a name is that?"

"Before we get to the cult, tell me about your relationship with her father."

She made a face.

"You mean you haven't heard of Del Richards?" It was a facetious question, meant to suggest that most of the public *did* know about her ex-husband. She said, "Del Richards is, has always been, and always will be an entrepreneur. He's bankrolled Grade Z teen horror movies. He's the only man I know who owns a ghost town. Oh, yes. He's roamed the West as a treasure-hunting enthusiast. He owns property across the border down in Kino Bay, well off the tourist track, and he's got a rep as an expert scuba diver, surfer, and fisherman. He dabbles in real estate. Everyone likes him, or at least pays him respect. Or pretends to. Tell me when to stop."

"Is he a nice guy?"

"No. Long ago when I first met him and he was just starting out, maybe then. He was nice to me. Then Janine was born and . . . well, screw the past. Live in the moment, right?"

"So what is the state of your relationship? Will it have any impact on my job?"

"It already has. Del knows that I retained your agency. I told him about it."

"And?"

"He's concerned about Janine too. It's the only thing we have in common anymore. You can form your own conclusions about Del. When I told him what I'd done, that I'd hired a detective agency, that I was driving in and getting a room and seeing what I could do about Janine, well, I expected him to give me resistance. But guess what?"

"What?"

"He approves. He wants you to drop by his place after you leave here, before you get started. I told him that was okay with me. Uh, is it okay with you?"

I said, "Hard to imagine what will be worse. Your ex-husband taking an adversarial position and mucking things up for me right from the start or him wanting to throw in and help out so he can really just keep a close eye on me. Either scenario is unacceptable."

"There's a third."

Beauregard seemed to have fallen asleep in her lap. She ceased tummy-scratching him long enough to brush back into place an errant strand of hair from her forehead and that was enough for Beauregard's eyes to pop open. He pawed her hand until she resumed scratching, whereupon his mutt eyes closed and he returned to his snooze.

Marna said, "Del just wants to check you out. Since the day Janine was born, he's been dictatorial and protective in equal measure. It's a matter of him needing to personally approve and that's okay with me. I've been out of their lives longer than I care to admit."

"What brought you back?"

"They say the death of a parent causes you to reassess your life. I guess that's what happened to me after Mom died."

"Tell me about Janine."

"Well, where to begin? She is . . . she *was* a

gymnast. She showed real talent for it from the time she was a little girl. You couldn't stop her from doing cartwheels and roundabouts."

Marna proceeded to expound on this, and the telling involved tangents, such as Janine's stellar school grades and her love of athletics, which resulted in Marna's moist eyes and tears as if she was eulogizing someone who no longer existed. I occasionally had to steer her back on course.

A coach in junior high mentioned to Marna that her daughter should start taking gymnastics lessons. Soon the child was sleeping in her jersey on Friday nights in anticipation of Saturday morning gymnastics class. Her big break came when she was spotted by the famed Olympics coach Boris Temerov who, during the Cold War, had defected to the United States from Bulgaria where he had trained seven female Olympic gold gymnasts. Recognizing the makings of another winner in Janine, Temerov had offered his services without charge if the girl would move to Atlanta and train at his facility.

It had not been an easy decision for the girl or her parents, but her drive had won the day. According to Marna, her daughter had no intention of spending the remainder of her life knowing that she *could* have gone to the Olympics, always carrying with her the curse of *what if*. So Janine's schooling was put on hold. She was packed off to Atlanta to study with the master. Temerov was a stern, humorless, controversial taskmaster. The sports media and insiders who accused him of pushing "his girls" too far often decried his harsh Eastern European approach.

Marna had tried to understand. Grueling, yes. It

was boot camp hell for her daughter, working with such a fierce trainer. But he was a great motivator. Marna saw her daughter blossom into a world-class athlete under Boris Temerov's tutelage. The balance beam was Janine's favorite event.

But Janine never made it to the Olympics. She never made the team.

This was the part of her story that generated the most emotion, causing Marna to pause several times to dry her eyes and clear her throat.

There was trouble at the training facility. Big trouble. *Janine's coach began visiting her in the middle of the night.* Things went to hell pretty fast after that.

Janine had always been a bright, vivacious girl, her mother told me, but the girl had always had "a dark place" concealed deep beneath the discipline of athletic achievement.

"It's a dark space at her core and she won't let anyone in," is how Marna put it. "Not even me, her own mother. We were fine when she was a little girl but as she began growing into a young woman, well, I tried. I really did, McShan. But a gulf grew ever wider between us. A lot of listening to headphones and then silent sulking if I instructed her to take them off at the Sunday table.

"Everyone was blindsided by the scandal. Temerov's people were able to keep it away from the media. Janine didn't want to press charges or testify. Del, of course, was another story. After Janine was back home and he found out the details of what happened, he promptly flew across the country to Atlanta before anyone knew what he was doing and beat Temerov to within an inch of his life. They kept that out of the media too." Marna gave a small smile. "You're a patient soul to be such a good listener, Mr. McShan."

"A private eye courtesy," I said.

She dug out her cell phone to check the passage of time. She cursed mildly under her breath and replaced the phone in her pocket.

"Time sure does drag when you're pouring your guts out. I need a cigarette. I tell myself I'm doing all of this, hiring you and all the rest, to help my daughter if she needs help. There's just something about the word 'cult' that I don't like. It's just sort of creepy, don't you think?"

"It can be."

"You've got to understand what my intention is. I want to put things back on track between Janine and me. My mother and I, well, there were the usual generational gaps here and there but we were never at each other's throat the way Janine and I get and we never stayed distant from each other the way Janine and I do. Mom was a good mother and I tried to be a good daughter. I want it to be that way between me and my kid."

I said, "I'll do what I can. I'm qualified to help out with misbehaving offspring. Working miracles, not so much."

She reached over to grace my forearm with a fingertip-light touch.

"It does sound like I'm laying a lot on you, doesn't it? But I'm not. I sense that you're a man who does things your way and that the confidence you exude has been earned through experience."

"You have a way with words."

A mild shrug caused brief movement under her blouse that I pretended to ignore.

She said, "I've played with flash fiction. I'd like to be a writer, but doesn't everybody? I just want you to know what you're stepping into."

"Then tell me what happened after Janine got home. After your ex cleansed the family honor by trouncing Temerov."

She said, "The sexual abuse of my child—yes, yes, I know all about statutory rape but whatever the shrinks and the lawyers call it, it damaged my little girl. Yes, she always had that dark space deep inside that she could withdraw into but that had always been a rare thing. It wasn't only her athletic skills but her drive, her determination that got her noticed. Always bright-eyed and beaming. But after Atlanta, well, the phone stopped ringing. Even old friends here in Arizona gave us the cold shoulder. Then it got worse.

"Janine got hooked on drugs. We didn't mind the pot at first, but she started drinking and Del found coke on the floor of her car one morning after she'd almost totaled it. I'm not proud of the role I played. I was drinking too much. My beautiful dream family had turned into victims and rage and dope . . . I dealt with it by numbing myself, by climbing inside a bottle. A classic drunk, that was me, and I didn't clean up until I checked myself into rehab. But by that time, I was in as bad shape as my kid. Like I said, we're two of a kind, my daughter and me, and that's not a good thing. Two birds without a nest. And that really sucks.

"From what I hear, Del has kicked Janine out of the house after he found her going into his safe to loot the petty cash. There was about a year when none of us were even talking to each other. The dysfunctional family in the flesh! Del filed for a divorce, and I signed off on it. I was glad to be on my own. Janine started tagging me for money but after a while that stopped when I started asking too many questions. She and her dad haven't patched things up all the way yet. I'm not sure of the details because Mom the gypsy hasn't been part of that. Until now." She squeaked out a small smile. "Now the bitch is back. Any more questions?"

I rose to my feet. Beauregard perked up in Marna's lap, his eyes bright and ready for anything.

I felt the same way.

I said, "I'll need your daughter's address, and directions to your ex-husband."

Chapter Four

I followed the State Highway west out of Bisbee, traveling along the U.S.-Mexican border toward Sierra Vista, a military town thirty minutes away, a suburban sprawl with a population of fifty thousand, crouched at the foot of the Huachuca Mountains.

Driving through open country under a blue sky with the AC on and practically no traffic to contend with, it felt good to be back in Arizona. This was my seventh visit to the state. I'd gotten to know this part of Arizona pretty well.

I'm not talking about anywhere north of Tucson: Phoenix, the Grand Canyon, Flagstaff. I'm talking about the 100-mile-deep strip of flyover country that runs along the border, in particular the southeastern corner of the state, Cochise County. These southernmost borderlands are Big Sky country where a soul can breathe. I felt it the first time I set foot out here and my fondness for the region had only grown over the years.

It's a land of open prairie and rugged mountains. Pockets of 21st Century civilization dot the land, and everyone's got a cell phone, but beyond town limits the vistas sweep clear to the distant horizon, interrupted only by stark mountain ranges lush with pine. Many have been drawn to these lands. Free spirits like the artist Georgia O'Keefe and the writer D.H. Lawrence, and those countless generations of everyday people following the sun since the days of the wild west and before. It's a hard, tough land with a fragile beauty that ranks as the most beautiful I've seen—the colors, the changes of the seasons, daybreak and sunset.

I could write a brochure for the Chamber of Commerce. Yeah, it felt good to be back.

The desert will either chew you up and spit you out or will touch you in ways that are as deep and mysterious as they are difficult to express.

Not far out of Bisbee, off to my left, was a wide expanse of prairie. In the distance, a stretch of the border wall, recently constructed by the Army Corps of Engineers, clearly delineated the Mexican/American border. Seen from this higher elevation and distance, it didn't look like much for stemming a human tide. Like trying to hold back a tsunami with a toothpick. History has taught that mass human migration is generally borne of necessity and so takes on an unstoppable momentum of its own. Pharaoh wasn't able to stop the Israelites, and it hardly seemed likely that a single wall will stop Mexicans and South Americans from seeking their piece of a dream that's been attracting immigrants to America since the Mayflower.

The highway traversed a wide swath of Sonoran desert, carpeted in emerald green cover. The temp was in the mid-nineties under a hazy blue sky. By afternoon, conditions would be ideal for monsoonal thunderstorms. I crossed over the San Pedro, running high and muddy this time of year, at the crossroads community of Gila Springs. Towering dogwood trees marked the meandering course of the river that, from higher ground, threaded its way across the rugged land like a big green snake.

After Gila Springs, I slowed and watched for the turnoff Marna mentioned, near where the highway curved north to parallel the base of the mountains.

Del Richards's acreage was nestled a couple of miles along a gravel washboard road in an upcurve of mountain. The nearest home site was more than a quarter mile away in either direction. The house was not visible because of the way the road angled and curved.

Stone pillars supported an open iron gate. I drove up a gently curving driveway, lined with trees that were trimmed and straight. I looped past the front of the house. I could see no sign of anyone or of anything in the house or anywhere on the property. A Humvee and a red Corvette were parked before a double garage.

I braked to a stop in front of the house. I touched a bell push and could hear it chime inside. I thumbed it a time or two more, but no one came to the door. I left the porch and followed a flagstone walk leading to the rear of the house.

A repetitive, muted thudding sound grew discernible when I rounded the corner. No one in sight but I recognized the sound, even muted, thanks to time spent in gyms when I was a young man and thought I would be a fighter. A long time ago.

Someone was working a punching bag.

The rhythmic *punch!-punch!-punch!* drifted out

through an open sliding glass door that gave onto the patio. I went over and peered in to see a man, who could only be Del Richards, fiercely jabbing a suspended punching bag that was held steady for him by a well-formed, well-toned leggy blonde.

They wore trunks and T-shirt. She filled hers out a hell of a lot nicer than he did.

The man did cut an impressive figure. Had to be pushing fifty but there was no trace of flab on his bullish frame. Tall. Heavy through the neck and shoulders. Thick, wavy black hair, worn on the long side.

I placed the woman at no older than her mid-twenties. She possessed a youthful vibrancy and would jiggle all over every time one of his power-jabs struck the bag that she hugged onto from behind. She wore stiletto high heels. She saw me over one of his shoulders that rippled under his T-shirt as he threw punches.

He sensed my presence. The bag he'd been pummeling came to a stop. Before the girl stopped jiggling, he swiveled around. The boxing gloves remained raised to chest level, elbows cocked outward. He regarded me with angry eyes set in a strong, handsome face.

"Who the fuck are you and what do you want?"

The woman said, "Del, that's not polite."

A quick sideways glare from him zipped her lip.

"Did I speak to you?"

"No."

"Didn't I teach you the blonde bimbo rules? What's the first rule?"

"Don't speak unless spoken to."

The words slipped between gritted teeth.

"So there you go. So shut the fuck up." He

extended his arms. "Unlace me." He glared in at my direction. "I said, who the fuck are you and what do you want?"

"I'm working my way through college," I said. "I sell personalities. Sounds like you could use a new one."

"Is that supposed to be funny?"

"Only if you think so. If you're Del Richards, I was told you were expecting me. I'm McShan."

The woman removed his right glove. He flexed his thick fingers. The knuckles sprouted mini-tufts of black hair.

"Oh, yeah. Right. Okay, okay. Sorry, sport. Drifters come through all the time this close to the border. Keeps a fella on edge."

"Sure."

"Marna told me about you. You don't look like a private eye."

I thought about using the trench coat and fedora line again. I decided he wasn't worth it. I held up the thin leather packet close enough for him to inspect my credentials. The agency has us licensed in all fifty states.

I said, "Your ex-wife says you offered to help."

The blonde freed Richards from his left-hand glove. He flexed his shoulders. He snickered.

"So Marna's concerned about Janine. No surprise there. About fucking time. Janine calls me every day on her cell phone."

"I was under the impression that you and your daughter were estranged."

"Yeah, well, that's just my ex-bitch talking." He turned to his . . . well, she wasn't wearing a wedding ring but of course that doesn't mean a thing these days.

Anyway, he turned to the blonde and said to her out of the corner of his mouth, "Fetch me a beer."

She said, "Yes, baby," and turned to me. "Would you like—"

He cut her off.

"Forget about him. Go on. Fetch me my fucking beer."

She avoided eye contact with either of us.

She said, "Yes, baby," again, and her stiletto high heels clicked out of the room.

Richards eyed her departure until she was out of sight. He licked his lips with an audible, smacking leer.

"Damn. Those high heels sure do something for a woman's backside, wouldn't you agree, sport? Hell, I even make Sherry wear 'em when I got her flat on her back in the old sackeroo. That's a woman's place, right? Flat on her back. Leave 'em upright too long and they start getting ideas above their station." He chuckled a lewd, manly chuckle. "Ain't that right, sport?"

I said, "This guy, Birch Sunday. Anything you can tell me that I should know about him?"

"Hell, no. Me and the woman just flew in yesterday after that damn Marna called to tell me what she'd done, hiring you. My family lived in this house for twenty years. I like it here. But the money's in L.A. so what are you going to do? Truth is, I don't know shit about this cult my little girl's gotten herself tangled up with. She was never the same after that Olympics mess. I guess Marna told you all about that."

"She did. Now it's your turn. That is if you want to help."

He faced me squarely. Started rubbing the knuckles of his right hand into the palm of his left.

He said, "Janine grew up in this house. I'll tell you what I tell her every time she brings it up. Truth is, if that little girl of mine is old enough to make a big mistake, then she's old enough to undo that mistake and set it right. She is not coming home, if ever, until she gets her head straight. So I'm going along with Marna about bringing you in. I'll let Janine come home again but it's going to be on my terms."

"Daddy's way or the highway?"

He nodded emphatically.

"That goes for anyone else too."

The blonde got me off the hook with the *click-click* of returning high heels. She sashayed in, handed Richards a bottle of imported beer. He took the bottle in one hand and slid his other around her trim waist, drawing her to him.

He said, "Another thing. You can tell that ex-wife of mine, if she doesn't already know it, that she's been permanently replaced." His right hand brazenly palmed Sherry's right breast through her T-shirt. "Replaced by a younger model that's nothing but a top shelf machine." His hand released the breast and slid back down to deliver a resounding slap to her firm behind. He said, "Men judge a man by the woman at his side."

The blonde said, softly, "So do women."

His eyes narrowed.

"So, McShan. How is it you plan to help my daughter?"

"First I'll have to determine if she needs help." I set my card on a counter where they could see it. I said, "I'm staying at the Copper Queen in Bisbee."

"I guess you know Janine's got herself a room at the cult site."

"Her mom gave me that information."

"Birch Sunday inherited acreage that includes a played-out copper mine, including what's left of the administrative building which he made into his headquarters."

"I'd have thought the big pit mine operation in Bisbee would have dominated copper production around here."

"It did, but the mine on Birch Sunday's land was an ISR mine. That's In-Situ Recovery. Drill boreholes in a deposit and artificially dissolve the minerals. Less costly way to mine low-grade copper ore. Stuff like that, it's sort of a pet interest of mine you might say."

"So your ex told me."

He chuckled.

"That woman does know me better than anyone. Must be why she hates me so much. And even that woman doesn't know everything about Del Richards. Not even close. I play my cards close to the vest in all things." Again, the manly chuckle. "All right, sport. I've had my look. You seem formidable enough. This time of day you're likely to find Janine at a place called The Dos Pesos."

"I passed it on my way here."

"If she's not there, you'll find her at the cult."

"Have you spoken with her today?"

"I have."

"Does she know about me, and why I'm here?"

"Not yet. Goodbye, McShan. Go earn your keep." Another slap jiggled the blonde's ass. "I'm in the mood for some relaxation. Come on, doll."

He led her out. Leading her, I noticed, by the wrist rather than holding her hand. A real romantic guy.

Sherry sent me one glance that came and went too quick for me to read. Then she lowered her eyes and allowed herself to be led from the room.

Chapter Five

The Dos Pesos, set back and separated from the highway by its parking lot, was opposite the school grounds in Gila Springs.

I parked the Jeep Wrangler at the end of a short line of customers' vehicles. Mostly pickup trucks, some with faded Trump bumper stickers. The place was doing a brisk business for being in the middle of nowhere.

The community, it was an exaggeration to call Gila Springs a town, was situated on a stretch of narrow flatland east of the San Pedro River. There were any number of these small crossroads communities dotting the state and county highways of rural Arizona. Places with names like Palominas, Hereford, Whetstone, St. David. Some incorporated, most not; meaning that some have the semblance of a small police force while for the most part these communities fell under the jurisdiction of the County Sheriff.

Gila Springs did not have a stoplight. There were a few weathered stop signs for shaded gravel roads that were lined with modest residences: manufactured homes and one-story adobe structures with wood frames. The restaurant was flanked by a closed-up gas station and a couple of vacant storefronts and *Johnny's Barbershop*. There was the fenced-in brick schoolhouse across the highway. Except for the barbershop, The Dos Pesos was the only commercial enterprise in sight.

I lowered my window and killed the Jeep's engine.

The heat was intense. You always hear them talking about the dry desert heat. That's true enough except during the monsoon season. Today's humidity was rising right along with the temperature. A thin stretch of thunderheads was gathering along the far southern horizon. The heat hammered into the vehicle as soon as the air conditioning quit. I turned the key, raised the window and let the AC resume.

Picnic tables sat in the shade of towering ash and cottonwood trees in front of the restaurant. Nearly all the tables were occupied. The clientele looked to be local, spanning the spectrum of age. Lots of denim and wide-brimmed hats. In these parts, "local" included any number of lifestyles. Ranchers. Off-duty soldiers from Fort Huachuca. A small posse of Hispanic teenagers, smoking cigarettes and looking macho in their baggy gangsta-rap jeans, caps worn askew and their wife-beater T-shirts. A sprinkling of moms, traveling in pairs most of them, carpooling and stopping for a snack on their way to or from errands and the Super Walmart in Sierra Vista.

Janine shared a table with a young man who was in his mid-to-late twenties. They were engaged in earnest conversation, which, from their emphatic gesturing and body language, I took to concern the sheaf of papers between them on the table. A pair of tall glasses, some kind of soft drink, held the papers in place against a warm breeze.

I saw her mother's beauty in Janine's features, but the kid hadn't done much with it. Her blonde hair fell limply to her shoulders, brushed but a dull yellow, not particularly cared for. She wore jeans, a shapeless T-shirt and no makeup. She was barefoot.

The young man with her had dark curly hair kept in place with some sort of grease. Harry Potter glasses. Chubby. A mild case of acne. Probably thought he was well-turned out in a pressed burgundy shirt worn open at the neck, pressed slacks and loafers. Not quite urban, not quite country. I would have noticed him in this bunch even if he weren't sitting across the table from Janine.

The sounds of children at play carried from the playground across the highway, interrupted at regular intervals by the *whoosh* of a passing vehicle. A black and white squad car, occupied by one of Gila Spring's finest, sat in a patch of shade on the school side of the road. The uniformed officer was munching a sandwich.

Over by the barbershop, a man stood in the doorway of the shop, his arms folded before him, leaning nonchalantly against the doorframe. Medium height. Slender. Quietly dressed.

In front of the barber shop, a Hispanic woman of Amazonian proportions straddled a Harley-Davidson Softail, finishing off what looked like a taco. She wore biker leathers that showed off the loud tattoos on her tawny arms. Arizona doesn't have a helmet law. Raven black hair glistened, worn long, wavy in the sunlight.

They gave the impression of disinterested observers.

I started to ease open my door. Seeing all those restaurant patrons at the outdoor tables, everybody enjoying themselves, reminded me that I could use some lunch. I paused, though, when things started happening between Janine and her lunch companion.

The guy in the burgundy shirt picked up the papers from the table and waved them in her face, saying something I couldn't hear, his expression twisted into a sneer, seen even from a distance.

Curious heads were turning from the neighboring tables.

Janine rose abruptly. She swiped the papers out of his hand and angrily crumpled them into a ball. She threw the wad of papers in his face. He stood. He started to say something. Janine mouthed angry words. Then she picked up one of the tall glasses and flung its contents in the guy's face.

There's only one thing a man, any man, can do at that point, excluding of course the socially unacceptable response of returning the favor. No, this young chap was well mannered enough, though his expression radiated fury. Too late to avoid making a scene, what with the soft drink soaking and darkening the front of his burgundy shirt, he simply hurried away.

Janine remained standing, glaring after him.

A few seconds later, a Ford Fiesta backed out from between two pickup trucks. I jotted down the license plate number. Rental tags. The compact zoomed off down the highway.

I could have followed, of course, and I thought about it. But if the guy in the burgundy shirt and Harry Potter glasses was important, I'd get another chance at him soon enough. I wanted to keep an eye on the misbehaving daughter, so I settled back to see what would happen next.

A waitress, a girl of about Janine's age, came over and appeared sympathetic and solicitous.

Janine had gotten some droplets of splash-back from the thrown soft drink. She dabbed at herself, assuring the server that she was fine. She paid her tab and started from the restaurant, only to find the three young thugs—they're called *cholos* along the border—blocking her path.

Words were exchanged. I couldn't hear the words but I could imagine. Their expressions and the body language when she drew up to face them indicated random idiot machismo rearing its ugly, stupid head. The sort of tired male bullshit every woman has to deal with from time to time, even here in this pristine near-wilderness. Words spoken with a swagger by the *cholo* who took one step ahead of the others, strutting his leadership position. Words spoken by Janine of the, "Aw c'mon, guys, let me pass," variety. She held a small backpack against her chest with both hands like a talisman.

Across the highway, the police cruiser remained in the shade by the schoolyard. The officer finished his sandwich. He was watching but made no move to intercede.

This time I did get the Jeep's door all the way open. I was about to step out and lend Janine a hand.

The full-throated roar of the Harley-Davidson motorcycle throttling to life filled the air. Everyone's attention, including mine, shifted in the direction of the barbershop. The Hispanic Amazon rode her hog at little more than an idle across the short distance. She booted down the kickstand, dismounting right where the *cholos* were hassling the girl.

What the hell.

I eased the door shut. I settled back, curious to see what would happen next. What Gila Springs, Arizona lacked in population, it more than made up for in entertainment.

The *cholo*-in-charge hesitated. His buddies drew back a few paces.

The big girl had to be six-feet-plus. Curvaceous as hell. Heavyset and all of it muscle. She snarled something. Then she delivered a powerful side kick. The toe of her boot caught the kid right between the legs. He doubled up and would have dropped but for the fact that she caught him. With one smooth, continuous and seemingly effortless motion, she hoisted the *cholo* high overhead with both arms. She flung him at his amigos, who toppled under his incoming weight like a line of bowling pins.

The Amazon had a sense of style. Without glancing around, but surely knowing everyone was watching her, she brushed her hands together a couple of times, signifying 'So much for that.' She didn't even glance in Janine's direction but strutted back to her bike, gunned it to life and executed a tight U-turn, returning the short distance to the barbershop where the barber stood waiting, leaning nonchalantly against the doorframe of his business. The big gal parked the bike. She and the man disappeared into the shop.

Janine sidestepped the cluster of *cholos*, wearing the tight expression of someone who just wanted to be gone from there. The *cholo*-in-charge lay curled up in a fetal ball on the ground, puking. His pals were doing their best to recover their thug cool after having been clobbered by a woman. The cop in the black and white on the other side of the highway was grinning. Janine, in her eyes-ahead, single-minded beeline away from the restaurant, managed to angle directly past the Jeep Wrangler.

My observer status had come to an end. I lowered my window.

I said, "A lover's quarrel and saved by a biker chick all in one day. Janine, you are a very interesting young woman."

Chapter Six

S he froze at the sound of her name. She regarded me with wary eyes. It was a child's face. Spilling blonde hair. Attitude to spare. A face that hadn't been lived in.

She said, "Buzz off, jerko. I don't know how you know my name, but I don't do pervs," and she started to walk away.

I said, "Your father told me where to find you."

She froze. Turned to face me.

"And why would anyone want to find me?"

I indicated the seat next to me. "Why don't you slide in?"

"Why should I?"

The wary eyes appraising me were clear. Not the eyes of a drunk or a druggie. They sized me up exactly as her mother had.

I said, "I'm guessing lover boy at the restaurant was your ride. I can give you a lift."

"Oh, like where?"

"Like wherever you want to go."

She processed that, then made up her mind.

"I'm going to miss afternoon service at the ranch if I don't get a ride." She rounded the front of the Jeep Wrangler. She climbed aboard and said, "But just so we get things straight, whoever you are. What you saw back there between me and Stan. Lovers' quarrel?" She gave an unladylike snort. "In Stan's dreams, and I doubt even there." She ignored the seatbelt and resumed her study of me. She said, "Who the hell are you?"

I told her my name.

I said, "I'm guessing the ranch I'm taking you to—"

She said, "Duh. The Spirit Ranch," and gave me directions.

I slipped the Jeep into gear and began to follow her directions. The police car pulled a U-turn in my rearview mirror and followed. I saw no reason to mention this, and Janine was too concerned watching me to check her outside rearview.

She said, "So . . . my father hired you?"

"No."

"I'll bet."

"It's the truth. Not on good terms with Dad?"

"I hate his guts. He's a control freak and a dictator. A user. So Mom hired you."

"Do you hate her guts too?"

She considered that. Thoughtful replaced petulance.

At her direction we caught a county road heading north along the river. The police car turned after us, maintaining tracking position three or four car lengths behind.

Janine was saying, "I'm too much like my mother to judge her. I'd feel like I was judging myself. We're too much alike for either of us to be fair-minded on the subject of the other."

I said, "That's fair."

"Sure it is. So rah-rah for me. Any more questions and you can let me out. What are you, a detective or something? Aren't there laws against people like you snooping around and screwing up people's lives?"

I said, "If there's not, there should be. But I'm not here to screw things up, Janine. Maybe I can help. From what I heard you do a pretty good job screwing up your life without anyone's help."

Her features twisted into a surge of rage. She drew back her right hand with the obvious intention of delivering an open-palmed slap across my chops. As if I was just going to sit there and let this little thing wale away on me. Without releasing the wheel with my left hand, my hand right clamped her wrist.

No slap.

She struggled to free her wrist, twisting and turning in her seat.

"Let me go, damn you. Let me go!"

I held firm.

I said, "I don't like violence."

"Okay! Let me go!" I held her wrist an extra few seconds to make my point. When I released her, she drew back against her door and eyed me like an injured child, massaging the wrist.

She said, "I didn't screw up! I didn't get to the Olympics because I was a fool for love instead of competition." She shifted her gaze to beyond the windshield, sighting in on some distant horizon. "Boris

Temerov was gentle. He was caring. Loving. I was lonely and upset and stupid. He was gentle."

"And Birch Sunday?"

"What do you know about Birch and me?"

"Not much. That's why we're talking."

She said, "Birch Sunday is a great man who's found wisdom through traveling a hard road. He's a wise man. A teacher."

"Like Boris?"

A chill descended between us. She eyed me for at least a half minute without saying anything. That's a pretty fair span of time to pass between two people driving down a country road.

Then she said in a level voice, "I don't think I like you, McShan. I think you're a creep."

I said, "So the guy who got a drink thrown at him isn't a sweetheart. What about the leather girl that just helped you out with the *cholos*?"

She said, "What, now you think I'm Yolanda's girl-friend? You *are* a perv. That had nothing to do with me, what you saw happen back there. Those thug wannabes asked for it and Yolanda gave it to 'em. She was letting everyone know that this is her turf. Anyone crosses Johnny the Barber, Yolanda takes 'em down. Anyone gets roughed up around here, she'll do it. Not a bunch of candyass *cholos*."

I thought of the guy in the barbershop doorway.

"Does the barber run a criminal enterprise in old Gila Springs? Do the cops know about it?"

She shrugged.

"What's there to know? The word is he'll guide in a load of migrants for the coyotes now and then. Run a little dope. Hot cars for a chop shop south of the line.

Yolanda? She's into girls but trust me, she doesn't even know I'm alive."

"So she was protecting her turf, not your honor?"

"She never said a word to me. Mister, I like boys."

That's when the cop who'd been following us switched on his rooftop light and gave one brief burst of his siren in case I wasn't paying attention.

The siren got Janine's attention.

She said, "Aw, shit," when she glanced in her outside rearview. She twisted around to confirm through the Wrangler's rear window. She said something worse. Only one word. Worse, that is, if you're as easily shocked as I am by a nineteen-year-old girl having a locker room vocabulary.

That's me. Old school.

I brought us to a stop at the side of the road and lowered the window.

The officer was forty-something. Khaki uniform, badly wrinkled. Smokey hat. Big hands and a loose mouth. Pale blue eyes, buttressed by discolored pouches, set close together in a flat, expressionless face. He leaned down and spoke past me, at Janine.

"Miss, are you all right?"

She sat with her arms folded, addressing the windshield instead of looking at either of us.

She said, "Yes, I'm all right," in a terse, bitchy small voice.

"Both of you, step out of the car, please."

I said, "What seems to be the problem, officer?"

"Step out of the car, sir. You too, miss."

No more *please*. Hand on his gun.

We did as instructed. He ordered Janine to stand behind my vehicle, behind me. His name tag under his badge read *Fusco*. He made a production of going through my credentials.

He said, "Private investigator. Huh. Licensed to carry a gun. Huh."

I said, "Why were we pulled over? I was going the speed limit."

He returned my credentials.

"I stopped you because you're not from around here. Winter is our tourist season. Snowbirds are long gone. You stood out." He indicated Janine. "I've seen her around. One of Birch Sunday's flock. Bunch of dumb-ass kids, if you ask me. I seen her jump into your vehicle with you and take off. Could be prostitution. Could be kidnapping. Maybe drugs. Thought I'd tail you for a spell."

"You weren't much concerned about that tussle back at the restaurant."

He didn't appreciate that, but the only indication was a single nervous twitch that tightened the corner of his left eye.

"I'd have stepped in if I thought it was necessary."

"But why spoil a good show?"

He ignored that.

He said, "You watch your step around here, private dick. I reckon it's your job to stir things up, ain't it?"

"Depends on the job."

"Yeah, well, might be a good idea to cancel this job, whatever it is, and head back to wherever it is you came from. That's just a piece of friendly advice."

He actually tipped his hat brim to me. He returned to his cruiser, executing a tight Y-turn and driving off down the gravel road.

Officer Fusco had not bothered to tell me that,

while my back was turned, he'd allowed Janine Richards to slip away.

She was nowhere in sight.

She was, as the old-timers in Arizona would say, flat gone.

Chapter Seven

I didn't spend time searching around for Janine. The GPS informed me that I was only a quarter of a mile from the entrance to The Spirit Ranch. Where else would she be headed? I drove the distance.

I found myself thinking about Janine's mom. I thought about the inner strength of a timid soul. Undertaking a journey through the South, spreading her mother's ashes. Befriending a little homeless mutt on the road. Resilience. A caring spirit. Open to the uncertainties this world serves up on a regular basis. Embracing life even if it meant having to pass eighteen wheelers on the interstate.

It's difficult to get anything going with an interesting woman in this life I lead. Fact is, I'd grown comfortable in my life and wasn't sure I'd know how to fit a woman into it. But hell, you've got to start somewhere. Marna was pure spirit packaged in a soft-spoken manner. Sort of naïve and yet direct. Easy on the eyes, too. If the opportunity presented itself, I intended to ask her out on a date when this was done.

The Spirit Ranch had no security. It wasn't that sort of place. A well-maintained gravel road curved off from the county road and crested the top of a hill that had been landscaped. A cluster of buildings baked under a worn sign, pockmarked with age and bullet holes, which read *The Consolidated Mining Company*. Cicadas chirped. Birds sang and wheeled about mulberry and juniper trees. Ancient mining machinery, hunkered beyond the landscaped grounds, provided a subtle reminder that this had once been a busy, industrious place.

A dozen vehicles, ranging from SUVs to mud-flapped pickup trucks to economy cars, were grouped before a one-story concrete building that had probably been the general office HQ for the old mine. I found a parking space. Three men and two women, casually attired, nodded a greeting to me while in the process of snubbing out their cigarettes and re-entering the building.

I had arrived in time for the afternoon service.

Inside, the building had a musty, echoing ambience where once the cacophony of typewriters, adding machines and mine business had reigned. The place didn't appear to have been renovated much but it had been kept up more or less. A wing of the building reached out in either direction from the entrance hall.

Nearly a dozen people in their early to mid-twenties, bearded males and their long-haired female counterparts clad in the contemporary casual dress of their generation, were in the process of migrating toward an open wide doorway opposite the main entrance. Their chatting back and forth suggested that former offices had been transformed into living quarters. Reminded me of a hippy-era commune.

A half-dozen individuals were already congregated in a big, white, high-ceilinged room that once would have been home to a massive secretarial pool. Nothing fancy or pretentious about the room or those present. Rows of metal folding chairs had been set up. Steel-casement windows filled the interior with comfortable daylight. Overhead fans dissipated the mustiness.

No sign of Janine.

I spotted Stan across the room. The squirrelly guy must have driven directly here from *The Dos Pesos*. He was keeping to himself. No mingling for him. He wore the same burgundy shirt. You couldn't tell that he'd been recently baptized with a drink. Evaporation doesn't take long in Arizona. He stood near the front of the small crowd, facing a podium that had a peace sign affixed to its front. Stan stared at his shoes and not much else.

Friendly, low-keyed conversation rippled through the room. A few of those present introduced themselves to me. There was Larry and Linda, a bright young couple, recently married and house-sitting over by Sonoita. And Fred, an older retired guy. Ex-military. Crazy about the year-round golfing. And Danni, a perky young mother from Tombstone. Nice, everyday country people.

Janine walked in. If she noticed Stan or me, she didn't let on except to position herself near the front of the crowd but on the opposite side of the room from Stan.

A door opened behind the podium. A man

appeared. A reverent hush fell upon the room. Could there be any doubt that this was Birch Sunday?

I pegged him at forty or not many years past that. Height, five-ten. Medium build. Weight, one-seventy. Mileage lines set in tanned, not unpleasant features. A sprightliness of step. A sharpness of eye behind rimless glasses. Tie-dyed T-shirt. Faded, outdated bell bottom jeans and sandals. Flowing silver hair that fell onto his shoulders with full beard to match.

Birch Sunday would stand out in any crowd.

He closed the door after him and stepped behind the podium, gaining everyone's attention. He beamed a benevolent smile and gestured with both hands.

"Please, my friends. Be seated."

Everyone sat, some of the younger attendees along the wall, cross-legged on the floor. Janine and Stan were at opposite ends of the front row, while I settled in the middle of the second-from-last row in the back.

At first it was like a routine communal meeting. Structural concerns about one of the storage buildings. The vegetable garden committee reported that the garden was doing well. Birch Sunday asked a few new members to stand and introduce themselves.

Throughout, he cut an impressive figure, speaking in the smooth, conversational tones of an NPR host. With cult business out of the way, he seamlessly segued into extemporaneous remarks with the delivery of a practiced communicator, which was at odds with his appearance. No begging for money. No proselytizing. His was a motivational talk. His gaze swept over us as he spoke in that NPR voice.

"Consider a discarded newspaper blowing down the street. Used. Done with. Finished. Uncared for.

That sheet of blowing newsprint doesn't even care about itself. But what becomes of it? Where will it end? Tiny torn fragments of it will become woven into a bird's nest from whence new life will burst forth. That sheet of newspaper can be used to block out the cold from the cardboard box of a homeless person. The universe makes use of something thought useless. My friends, everything, *everyone*, has value. Our every experience is a spiritual experience. I observe the world and yet I trust my inner vision, allowing things to come and go, preferring what is within to what is without. The difference between 'living the dream' and 'caving under the pressures of reality' is perception. Perception, I say, *is* reality. Sacred is the gentle, healing light of this Truth."

I clocked him. He went on like that for nine-and-a-half minutes. He didn't overdo it. Birch Sunday held the rapt attention of his audience with his message and delivery.

When he was done, some drifted off as they had arrived, in twos and threes while some from the front row stepped up to engage Birch Sunday in conversation. He greeted them warmly. Folks were chatting up each other around the room while others were reaching for their car keys.

Stan had moved to stand just short of the double doors where he was overseeing a donation basket. I couldn't make out the denominations of the bills, but it was all paper money, no coins. Stan stared laser-like at the front of the room, at Janine. He ignored those who passed and dropped donations into the basket. Stan did not bother to nod appreciation or engage them in conversation. He had eyes only for Janine.

Janine continued to ignore him, though aware of him giving her the evil eye. Those around them didn't seem to notice. Janine refrained from approaching Birch Sunday while he was in conversation.

When I drew up next to her, she regarded me coolly.

I indicated Stan with a nod.

"I'm trying to decide if he's jealous."

Her mouth tightened into a severe line.

"I told you—"

We were whispering. No one overheard us.

I said, "Okay, don't get sore."

"And why would Stan be jealous?"

"Well, what about you and Birch?"

"What?"

I said, "You know."

She faced me squarely.

"Y'know something, dude? You're getting to be a stone pain in the ass, and I don't even know you. Private investigator." She made a derisive, snorting sound.

"Janine, you got here before I did. You split while Officer Fusco was busting my chops and he must've thought it was funny, letting you hightail it like that behind my back. You cut across on foot while I had to finish up with the law and drive over here."

"I'm sure this has a point."

"It does. When I got here, everyone was gathered, waiting for Birch. But not you. Then you show up, and so did he. Timing is everything."

She said, "You're a dirty old man with a dirty mind."

"What's that got to do with it? And what do you mean, old? I'm just telling you what everyone else saw.

So, were you and Birch alone together? Was I a topic of conversation?"

"I haven't told Birch a thing about you. Yet." She registered a small smile. "Tell you what. Let's set your mind at ease. I'll introduce you. Then you can stay the hell away from me and tell mother dearest that Birch Sunday and my friends here are fine, decent people and that I'm doing just fine, thank you very much."

Birch was winding up his conversation. A round of hugs and handshakes.

I said, "Leave out who I am. That'd be best for all concerned."

"Including me?"

"Especially you."

She took my hand and chuckled.

"This is no time to be shy, Mister P.I."

I allowed myself to be led by a nineteen-year-old.

Janine said, "Excuse me, Birch. There's someone I'd like you to meet."

Chapter Eight

B irch Sunday's handshake was firm. Big, healthy
smile.

"A pleasure to meet you, Mr. McShan. Welcome to
Spirit Ranch."

Janine said, "We just met McShan at The Dos
Pesos. Mr. McShan gave me a ride in."

That was an interesting thing for her to say for a
couple of reasons. For one, yes, she'd just met me, true
enough. But far from inviting me onto the Spirit Ranch
grounds, she'd given me the slip and left me on my own
to track her down. There was also the fact that, despite
being understandably irked at having a private detective show up in her life the way anyone would, here she
was less than an hour since our meeting, telling half-
truths on my behalf. Not mentioning that I was a P.I., as
I'd thought she would.

If Birch Sunday was aware that my ride offer was
precipitated by Stan running out on her at the restaurant, he gave no indication.

Birch said with a smile, "Thank you for bringing

Janine home, Mr. McShan. And you're more than welcome to make yourself at home. We keep vacant guest rooms available for overnight visitors. Spend the night with us here at the ranch, if you wish. Perhaps you'll decide to stay on here and join us. It happens."

I acknowledged the offer with a smile of my own.

"Birch," I said. "That's an interesting name. Sunday. Is that a family name?"

"An adopted last name. Out here in the West, Americans have been reinventing themselves for centuries. I am only one of millions. A common man who sought a new beginning and, with The Spirit Ranch, I can now provide that same opportunity for others. Here it matters not where you hail from. Your name. Your history. The god of your parents. All that a person may choose to leave behind so that a new life can begin, whatever they envision their destiny to be. Born here. This land, this work, is my life. My destiny. My dharma. It's all I want and it's all I have. I will never relinquish what I have found here, nor will I allow it to be taken from me."

"You sound determined. Is someone trying to take this from you?"

Some of his amiable warmth cooled.

"There are dark forces at work against me," he said. "Unmanned drone flyovers have been observed. And it's not Fort Huachuca training exercises, as the authorities claimed when I lodged a complaint. Did you know, Mr. McShan, that mining technology today allows for drones to survey the land?"

"And that's what's happening to you?"

A small shrug accompanied his reply.

"Who knows? And now . . . you."

"What do you mean, me?"

Long pause. Steady eye contact between us.

He said, "I see beneath artifice."

"Yeah, so do I."

He broke eye contact.

"You'll excuse me. It's been a strenuous day. It's time for my meditation. I practice deep breath meditation, Mr. McShan. I would urge you to do the same."

"And why would you urge that, Birch?"

Extended pause. Another healthy smile.

"Because I urge everyone here to meditate."

He all but wafted away on sandaled feet, exiting through the doorway behind the podium.

I started to say something to Janine.

She was nowhere in sight.

Maybe she thought it was funny, pulling that disappearing act twice in a row, but it irked me. Apparently, I'm really something when it comes to taking on bad guys with guns but pit me against a teenage girl with attitude and I'm lost.

No sign of Stan, either.

No sign of anyone except a young woman busy straightening the rows of folding chairs for the next gathering.

I could have snooped around. Heck, I'd been invited by the big cheese himself. The smell of cooking from somewhere nearby reminded that me I hadn't eaten since breakfast. I gave consideration to sticking around for dinner. I was feeling tired after no more than stolen sleep during the past twenty-four hours. But I'd learned and done enough for one visit.

On my way out, I snagged a brochure. I thumbed through it, a cursory glance. Apparently, Birch not only conducted "spiritual gatherings" twice a day, seven days a week he also scheduled "meditation activities" that included yoga classes and "meditation hikes". Did they meditate while they were hiking, or did they hike to a spot and meditate? The brochure didn't say.

I thought about things on my drive to Bisbee.

At this point, I was willing to give Mr. Birch Sunday the benefit of the doubt and accept for now that he was everything he appeared to be. In my line of work I've encountered more than my fair share of smooth-talking grifters who were so smooth, they could scam you out of anything if they put their mind to it. You have to admit, a remote ranch off a county back road was a sweet setup for any manner of illegal activity. A rural piece of land along the border with a fluid number of residents, coming and going. It was a setup for anything from hot cars to those things that had worried Marna Richards: white slavery, kidnapping, and of course the smuggling of drugs and guns.

The politicians in Washington always bring up border security during election cycles but the fact is that the southern border of the U.S. has been a porous security nightmare that hasn't seen an iota of change for centuries. In the 19th Century, big business smuggled in millions of undocumented Chinese immigrants to work building the transcontinental railroad. In the 20th Century it was liquor that was smuggled across during prohibition and, later, drugs. The border separating Arizona from Sonora, Mexico has always been a free-booter's paradise. The 21st Century was seeing a mass migration from the south of historic proportions.

If Birch Sunday was dirty, I wondered if he and Johnny the Barber were associates or competitors.

And now there was a fresh angle on Janine for me to consider. Why did she keep our secret about who I really was and why I was there? She'd had the opportunity to blow the whistle on me right there in front of Birch. When I understood what was going on between her and Birch Sunday, I'd know more of what I needed to earn Marna Richards's retainer.

At this point, though, I didn't know enough. The Poppy Kincaid case in Denver had only been the latest of the cult-oriented assignments I'd drawn from the agency. It's pretty codified by now, how a cult works. In the case of kids like Janine, when they join, they're generally searching to find and fill in a piece that's missing from their life.

In Janine's case, and in most of the cases I've encountered, it stems from a dysfunctional family. A troubled teen would be drawn to exactly the sort of group Birch Sunday had organized, to gain the "family" she felt she'd lost. But that wasn't the vibe I'd picked up on when Janine introduced me to Birch Sunday. There could be hanky panky going on between them despite her protestations to the contrary but, keeping Birch in the dark concerning my true identity, yes, that was a new angle to the "misbehaving daughter". Maybe there were things Janine wanted to know about Birch, and she was perfectly happy for me to do the digging.

I parked the Jeep Wrangler outside The Copper Queen. The sun was behind the hills. Color was in the evening sky. A restless night wind came down off the mountains. There were cloud banks to the south but no indication of rain.

I checked my phone messages. I try to stay up with the tech side of things. I really do. Nowhere near enough, though, to satisfy Ms. Agatha Honeycutt. As usual, there were a dozen texts. They grew increasingly terse and demanding, informing me that I was tardy in reporting in. I promised myself to call or text Agatha first thing in the morning.

The nice thing about cell phones is that, although intended to keep everyone in touch and plugged in twenty-four seven, the little buggers in fact provided a whole new set of believable alibis for dodging the callers you don't want to deal with, especially in the wide open spaces of the Great American West. "I couldn't get a signal," etc.

I did dial up Marna Richards. I was routed directly to her voice mail. One of those mechanical robot answering messages. I informed her voice mail that I had made contact with her ex-husband and with her daughter, and that her daughter was healthy and, so far, appeared to be in no immediate danger. I said that I would follow through and deliver a report the following day. Normally I'd have ended the message right there. For some reason, though, I tacked on: "Good night."

Okay, I'll cop to the smallest impulse of disappointment that she hadn't picked up. She and Beauregard were ensconced in their little tipi less than fifteen minutes away. Dinner or a nightcap together would have been nice. Or inappropriate? Damn if I understood the dance anymore. She was probably out walking Beau on his constitutional, turning off her phone to enjoy the peace and quiet.

Yeah, I'd call her tomorrow.

I strolled into The Copper Queen's ornate lobby and was halfway to the dining room when I was intercepted by Sherry.

She'd traded the stiletto high heels, T-shirt and trunks for tailored tan slacks, shoes with low heels that still managed to accentuate a swell figure and a black satin blouse that did the same.

There was no sign of Del Richards.

She greeted me with her restless energy channeled into a wide, gorgeous smile. It was apparent that she'd been waiting for me.

"Hi there, McShan! Had dinner yet?"

Chapter Nine

And so we had dinner together, Sherry and I.

She was a fine dinner companion. Flashier than Marna. More sass. That was her style, and she wore it well with the clatter of silverware and countless conversations prattling around us in the busy main dining room. The youthful vibrancy of earlier, that glowed despite her having to repress it around Del Richards, infused her now with tanned, healthy vitality. When she smiled, parted lips revealed beautiful teeth. She had a carefree laugh, and I could hardly help but admire her suppleness of figure.

Well, I was working a case and she was part of it. Sure, I enjoyed her company. Our small talk meandered from this subject to that, revealing in her a caring heart, a good head on her shoulders and a tart wit. Sherry had three glasses of wine. She was a girl who didn't mind having a good time.

Full name: Sherry Lynn Bostwick. Wisconsin girl. Janesville. Local beauty pageant winner. Married some local guy who managed his dad's hardware franchise. Found out she couldn't have children. Depression. Escape into TV and movies and Harlequin romance novels, which turned out to be a good thing, to hear her tell it. Her morphing of real life and make-believe resulted in a lost marriage and a solo move to L.A. to become an actress. She was waitressing in the Denny's on Sunset when she met Del, who determined upon first sight that she was perfect for the female lead in a movie he was producing and directing. Sherry knew upon first sight that all Del wanted was to get into her panties. But that was okay. That's how it was done. And so Sherry ended up third billed in an R-rated teen horror film that went straight into a DVD release that she refused to name.

"Del and I have been an item ever since."

"Married?"

She rolled her eyes and made a face.

"No, thank God."

"Sherry, are you baiting a trap for me?"

She tilted her head to the side and regarded me with a single arched eyebrow.

"Now what makes you say a thing like that?"

I thought of earlier; of Del leading her out of the room not by holding hands but with a dominant grip of her wrist.

I said, "I saw the way he treats you. Are you a masochist, Sherry? Do you like being treated like that?"

"Del has his ways."

"Okay."

"No, I mean he really is okay."

"Okay."

"Damn it, McShan, I drove all the way over so here we could spend some time together. You're an interesting guy, certainly capable of amusing and diverting dinner conversation. So why are you baiting me? Why?"

"I guess I'm impatient to know why you're really here."

"I've already told you—"

"I mean besides my charming dinner conversation."

Our waitress approached to clear away our dinner dishes.

When we were alone again, Sherry said, "Del lied to you."

"I was wondering about that. What did he lie about?"

"He said he and Janine spoke every day. That she calls him on her cell. That was true up until they had their big fight."

"About what?"

"I don't know. Del took pains to keep me from overhearing, but I could tell. But honestly, I couldn't make out what it was they were arguing about."

"Any idea?"

"No. Del never talks to me about Janine or Marna. Never. He was going through his divorce when we met, and I never pushed it. But he and his daughter haven't spoken since that big fight, whatever it was about. You saw what Del's like. He's drinking more. He's always had a mean streak but lately . . ."

She lowered her eyes. The words tapered off.

I said, "And all you have to do is study the bimbo rulebook."

She glared up at me.

"That was a shitty thing to say. It's been a lovely dinner, McShan. You've been so nice. Why stop now?"

I said, "You've been nice too. But I'm a paid snoop. You knew that when you came here. That's *why* you're here, isn't it?"

Her glare softened. The hint of a pretty smile.

"Don't be so sure, tiger."

"Stop it. Why did you come here to see me, Sherry? Really."

"Because I feel sorry for Janine, that's why. The kid's had a rough time of it for someone who hasn't even made twenty yet."

"Are you friendly with her?"

"Are you kidding? She probably hates me more than she hates her mother. No, I've hardly spoken with her. I see her once in a while from a distance. I feel sorry for her. McShan, I saw you go practically toe to toe with Del. Talk about a pair of alpha dogs. But you want to know something? You've got the edge because you're one of the good guys."

I said, "I'm just a working stiff. Are we having trouble with Del?"

She sighed.

"I don't kid myself. At first, I thought it was real love between us. I'm a romantic sort of girl. At first, Del was this handsome, well-built passionate lover who made movies and had all these wild hobbies. He was divorced and available. And he wanted me. And it's still there, McShan, God help me. There's some crazy physical *thing* between us. I'm thinking more and more that it's a bad habit that I need to break.

"I haven't left him . . . *yet*." She fidgeted with a napkin the waitress had overlooked. "I'm not proud of that, but you know how it is. If the sex is good, you find a way to make everything else work. If the sex isn't happening . . . forget it. There's something *primal* between me and Del. But I don't always like him. Recently it's turned from passionate to nasty and mean. As for his kid, well, she deserves the best and I've got a feeling you'll smooth it out that way for her, whatever's going on. So you deserve to know the truth. Or at least the truth as I know it. That's why I came to see you. Okay?"

"Thanks, Sherry. Maybe I can act a little nicer to you."

She liked that. She favored me with a hand squeeze across the table.

We encountered Del outside.

He was leaning against the hood of Sherry's snappy little red Corvette, his legs crossed at the ankles. Massive arms folded across his broad chest.

He said, "Well, well, here they are. Sorry I couldn't join you." His voice lowered to a growl. "But I wasn't fucking *invited*."

"Now, Del—"

He left the hood of the car. Straightened to his full height.

"Don't *now, Del* me. What the fuck is going on here?"

Sherry retained a cool demeanor.

That was good enough for me. It's been more than a couple decades since I was caught by a jealous husband. I was a young man, then. Hormones overruled common sense on a regular basis back in those days.

This was different. This assignment included defusing a volatile domestic situation.

So I just stood there.

Sherry rested a hand on each of his shoulders.

"Del, you've got nothing to be jealous about and you know it. I'm full grown and I can be trusted. Mr. McShan asked me to drive over here to discuss the case he's working for Marna. You were taking a nap and I didn't want to wake you so I—"

Del took firm hold of both her arms, above the elbows, and lifted her bodily several inches off the ground. He set her down by his side so that he and I were once again facing off.

He said, "You want to talk about the case, McShan, you talk to *me*. You don't slide around hustling my wife. Damn my ex and her crackpot ideas, bringing someone like you into this." He raised clenched fists. "Maybe I should knock your block off."

Enough was enough.

I said, "Maybe you should try."

Sherry retrieved a jingling set of keys from her purse.

"Boys. Boys. Behave! We're in public. And I'm going home." She unlocked the 'Vette and positioned herself behind the steering wheel.

Del sneered. "About time you did something right. Damn bimbo. I'll see you when I get home."

I heard myself say to Sherry, "Will you be all right?"

I couldn't help myself.

Del said to me, "Dial it back, sport. I look out for this woman, not you."

Sherry drove off.

Del had yet to break eye contact with me.

He said, "Stay away from her unless you want big trouble."

You have to let a man keep his pride.

I watched him stalk off. I watched his taillights follow those of the little red 'Vette's until they were out of sight.

Chapter Ten

The next morning, I awoke with the sun. Morning exercises. Shower, etc. I skipped shaving. A glass of OJ from the fridge while I dressed for the day.

I caught the local morning weather forecast on TV. Another scorcher, though a low-pressure system was moving in to bring with it a slight drop in record temperatures and an increased chance of rain. Arizona has got to be one of the only parts of the country where a weatherperson can say the words "one hundred degrees" and "cooling trend" in the same sentence.

Turned off the TV screen. Checked the phone screen. No return call from Marna. I had a couple of stops in mind to round out my picture of Janine's world. That would take me until around noon, at which time I'd give Marna a call if I hadn't heard from her by then. If she did call me first, I would recommend that we meet for lunch. I'd then deliver her my report on what I learned about her daughter.

My phone's screen listed another four calls during the night from Agatha Honeycutt. Those of us who were Agatha's "foot soldiers" often wondered how—or *if*—our commander-in-chief ever found time to sleep. I'd get back to Agatha after I spoke with Marna.

I am not of the screen generation. Doubt I ever will be. The Screen Generation. Studying. Relaxing. Reading. Communicating. Researching. Having sex, alone or with someone else. All of it on The Screen. Flat screen. Big or small PC monitor screen. Smart phone screen. TV wide screen. You don't have a screen? Friend, you're just not on the grid.

Like I said. Old school.

I drove to Gila Springs.

The morning was warm. The sky, a washed out blue. The atmosphere was juicy with a heavy mugginess.

The Dos Pesos was doing a modest breakfast business. I took an outdoor table that afforded me a clear view of Johnny's Barbershop. The *Closed* sign in the window was visible from this distance.

There was moderate traffic along the highway. Children could be heard playing in the schoolyard across the way. No sign of Officer Fusco in his black and white. Birds sang in the trees.

Took my sweet time over a tasty plate of *huevos rancheros*.

I tried resisting a small itch to call Marna. Business? Personal? Hell, I don't know. It was just an itch. One of those crazy impulses you get. I went ahead and dialed. Again, I got her voice mail. This time I didn't leave a message.

The phone piped out its electrical tune. The screen read *Agatha Hunnicutt*. I pressed random buttons until the cell phone's small screen went dark and then slipped the phone into my pocket.

A brand-new red diesel Chevy pickup drew up to the barbershop at exactly ten o'clock, followed by the flame-haired, leather-clad biker girl on her Harley. They parked alongside the barbershop. The driver of the pickup was the slender, compact guy who yesterday had observed the action from the door of his shop. When he stepped down from the cab, he appeared dwarfed by his vehicle. He unlocked the front door of his shop.

Yolanda followed him in.

I waited until the lights went on and the *Closed* sign had been turned around to read *Open*. Then I paid off my breakfast tab and walked the short distance to the barbershop.

When I reached the shop, Yolanda was bent over, polishing the chrome on her bike. Something told me that woman rarely missed anything going on around her, but for me she gave a fine performance of someone so busy at her task she never saw me when I strode past and entered the barbershop.

It was a one-chair shop. You can still find them along the back roads of rural America existing in an alternate reality, where words like "unisex" and "hair stylist" seem never to have been invented. A comfortable maleness dominated from the pleasant scents to the framed pictures on the walls. Everything but a spittoon. A hat rack stood in one corner. In this day of baseball caps worn everywhere, even to church and at the dinner table, when's the last time you saw a hat rack? Two unoccupied waiting chairs. A radio softly played a country music station. A TV mounted up in one corner was tuned to CNN with the sound off.

Johnny the Barber had surely observed my approach from the restaurant. When I stepped into his shop, he rose from the barber chair. A wide smile. Early forties. He had lovely white teeth that gleamed when he smiled.

"Good morning, sir."

"'Morning." I eased into the chair with my best top-of-the-morning smile. I said, "I'll take a shave and a trim."

"Yes, sir. Coming right up." He draped the barber cape over me. Clipped it behind my neck. He said, "Think we'll get us some rain today?"

He got to work. We made small talk. I relaxed, but not so much that I didn't let the fingertips of my right hand rest, under the barber cape, close to my right boot wherein resided my Glock 17 9mm.

I mean, come on. I was here to gather information and one of the primary question marks was presently working on me with a straight edge razor.

Johnny the Barber had a nice touch. Efficient. Professional. And he possessed that gift of easy gab that is the birthright of barbers and bartenders the world over. The weather was changing. I was just passing through, looking over the country, and visiting family in Tucson. We skirted politics. Yakked some on the price of local real estate which was on par for this part of the country. Ten minutes of that and he was removing the cape and brushing off my neck and shoulders.

I rose from the chair. I enjoy the feel of a fresh barbershop shave. I waited until he was handing over my change.

I said, "Del Richards said to say hello."

His brow furrowed in thought.

"Del Richards. Del Richards. Don't think I know that name, amigo. Is he from around here?"

"Raised a family just up the road. I thought the town barber would know everyone."

The smile didn't change but his eyes narrowed.

"I said I don't know him, amigo. Thanks for your business. You have a nice day now, hear?"

He went about shaking out and folding the cape.

I pocketed my wallet.

"Then I don't suppose you'd know his wife or their daughter, Janine."

"Amigo, you ask questions like a policeman."

"Ain't that something."

"You look for answers where there are no answers. Like Don Quixote, searching for what is not there."

I was stunned at the literary allusion.

"Cervantes, Johnny?"

"What? You think I can't read? You think I'm just a stupid Mexican."

It was time to dial it up a notch. To scratch beneath the surface of civility and see what I could find.

I said, "Can you blame me?"

The big Harley gal chose that moment to step into the doorway, leaning indolently against it. She eyed me up and down. She hadn't missed a word of our conversation.

"Be careful with this one, *mi hermano*." She spoke in a heavily accented contralto. "Let me take him. I hate smartass *cabrones*. I like to take them apart. Let me take him."

Johnny stood beside his barber chair. Yolanda blocked the doorway. They had me boxed in.

On the highway a semi geared down and rumbled past, shaking the windows.

Johnny said, "I think it is best for you to leave now, amigo."

Yolanda eased inside, positioning herself in front of the line of customer chairs by the window. Like many large people, she possessed a limber economy and grace of movement.

I said, "Okay, then. Until next time."

I made my way through the doorway, into the morning sunshine.

Yolanda called after me.

"Next time, cabrón, they *carry* you out."

Chapter Eleven

"*And so the prodigal son returns. At least on the telephone.*" Miss Agatha Hunnicutt was not pleased. There was a noticeable tremor to her voice across the connection that could only be attributed to festering rage. "*Awfully nice of you to check in.*"

I was driving down the state highway from Bisbee to Gila Springs.

I said, "Agatha, I need information."

"*I'll give you information. I'm that close to pulling you off the roll and sending another operative down there to take your place. How's that for information? Is that news you can use?*"

"Here's what I need—"

"*Hush up. I'm not done. You know I expect my foot soldiers to report on schedule. I expect punctual updates.*"

"From me? After all this time?"

"*Listen, you . . . you rebel. Don't you get smart with me. What information do you need?*"

I recited the license plate number I'd jotted down

yesterday of the car driven by Stan of the burgundy shirt and Harry Potter glasses.

"I'm guessing it's registered to a rental company. Sierra Vista. Tucson. Maybe Phoenix. A Ford Fiesta rented by someone I know only as Stan. Find out from his application who he is. Line of work. Business affiliations. Residency."

"What else? And there'd better be more, McShan, for all the time you've been down there."

"John Gallegos."

"What's a John Gallegos?"

"That's what I want to know. Everyone down here calls him Johnny the Barber."

"How do you know his real name?"

"I'm a detective. This is the sort of thing I'm trained to do. Got his name off his license on the wall. Johnny's got a rep down here as a slick dude. A player. Skirts the law. Breaks it when he can."

"And he's tied in with our client's daughter how?"

"That is to be determined."

"Okay. We'll dig up his B.G. Now listen to me, McShan. I want you to answer your phone when I or one of my assistants calls you back. understand?"

"Now, Agatha, don't get bossy."

"And why the hell not? I am the boss!"

"Trouble's brewing down here," I said. "I just ran into my first pushback. The suggestion of physical intimidation."

She chuckled.

"I love it when you talk dirty. But what does that mean, suggestion of physical intimidation?"

I didn't want to admit that I'd been threatened by a biker girl.

I said, "Look, the important thing is, when there's pushback like there just was, there's something they don't want found out. I want to find out what that is."

"Yeah. Now what about our client? Have you spoken with Mrs. Richards yet today?"

"Coming up. Gotta go, Agatha."

"Don't you hang up on me, boy, or I'll—"

I ended the connection. I shut off the phone. Back into my pocket it went.

The Spirit Ranch was basking in sun-splashed, pastoral, mid-morning peace and quiet when I parked in the same parking spot as on my previous visit. Birds sang from their trees. A breath of warm wind rattled the branches of the cottonwoods. A few people were about here and there but not as many cars in the gravel lot as yesterday. I recalled from the brochure that things started happening at the Ranch in the afternoon and evening.

A young man was pushing a broom around the room where yesterday's service had been held.

"Yes, sir?"

"'Morning. I'm looking for Birch. Is he around?"

"Uh, he is. But he's with the meditation group."

"Aw, c'mon. No way he can break away for just a minute?"

"Oh, definitely not. Birch is guiding the meditation."

"Ah, okay. Thanks."

"Have a nice day, sir."

"By the way, you haven't seen Janine around this morning?"

"Sure haven't. You have a nice day, sir."

He replaced his ear buds and resumed his brooming.

I'd wanted to chat up Birch away from Janine. I was interested in what he'd have to say about Johnny the Barber. It was still bugging me that Johnny and Yolanda felt compelled to be so damn touchy about my asking them questions. I also had a few questions about the mysterious Stan. But since this was not yet the time for that conversation, it *was* time for a report to Marna Richards.

I was walking out to my vehicle, reaching for my cell phone to give her a call, when out of the corner of my eye I spotted movement at an end of the main building.

A Ford Fiesta was parked over there, backed up to a side entrance. The trunk was open. Stan was in the process of positioning a suitcase there.

I closed the distance between us, catching him by surprise just as he slammed the trunk shut and started for the driver's side. When he noticed my approach he paused uncertainly, his hand resting on the door handle.

Stan had aged ten years since yesterday. There were discolored pouches under the eyes behind the Harry Potter glasses. His hair was rumpled.

He said, "Yeah, what is it?"

"Your name wouldn't be Glenn Hyatt, by any chance?"

He smiled nervously.

"Not me. Case of mistaken identity. Sorry, guy."

"From Tucson, Glenn W. Hyatt. Head Accountant. Winthrop, Jones and Willard. A general description that's out matches you to a T."

He started to get flustered.

"I don't know what you're talking about. That's not me." He opened the car door. "I've got to go."

I put an edge in my voice.

"For your sake I hope you're right because the guy I'm talking about made off with thirty-two thousand dollars in cash." I flipped open my leather folder to give him a fast glimpse of my credentials across the roof of his car. "Your identification, please."

Stan looked around as if hoping that someone in the immediate vicinity who knew him would step forward and offer assistance by confirming his identity. My luck held. There was no one in sight. With an exaggerated show of reluctance, Stan opened his wallet and extended his arm across the car's roof, providing me with a look at his driver's license.

I snatched the wallet from his hand. Why miss an opportunity to intimidate someone?

New Mexico license. Stanley V. Sweetson. Albuquerque. The picture on the license was terrible but it was the same guy.

I handed him back his wallet.

"Guess I made a mistake, Mr. Sweetson. I apologize."

Birch Sunday's voice said coolly, "Well, well, well. McShan the private detective, come to detect."

He stood in a doorway behind us, wearing a mildly curious smile.

Sweetson said, "You guys work it out. I'm out of here." He lowered himself behind the Fiesta's steering wheel and reached for the ignition.

I said to Birch, "How'd you find out I was a PI?"

"Janine told me. You didn't think a teenager could sit on a secret like that, did you?"

Two things happened at once.

A black and white police cruiser suddenly appeared, approaching at a high enough rate of speed to kick up a cloud of dust in its wake along the gravel road. No siren but the rooftop lights were flashing. The black-and-white skidded to a stop at an angle so as to block the Fiesta from leaving.

Officer Fusco emerged.

Sweetson bolted from his Ford Fiesta and took off running. An open stretch of rough ground separated the building from a line of trees beyond which the terrain dropped off in a steep slope. Stan Sweetson ran for that tree line fast as his pumping legs would carry him.

My reaction was reflexive, like a greyhound at the track when he spots the speeding mechanized bunny. I'm a manhunter by training and instinct. They run. I chase.

Stan was no match for me, but he did have a head start. I hustled around the car, and he must have heard me coming because he started running faster. I charged after him and was soon twenty paces short of grabbing him by the collar and taking him down.

A gunshot brought me up short.

The report made a dull *pop!* in the wide-open spaces, like a paper bag filled with air being popped.

"Hold it right there, McShan!" Then Fusco remembered his training and the cop films he must've been a rabid fan of. He shouted, *"Freeze!"*

I froze.

That's the difference between me and the average

citizen like Stan Sweetson. I am licensed to legally practice my profession. I can carry a concealed weapon. In return I am obligated to obey all federal, state and local statutes. Failure to do so would result in the suspension of my license. When an officer of the law instructs me to freeze, it behooves me to recognize his authority. And of course, it's always prudent to obey the commands of those with flashing lights on their vehicle and a gun in their hand.

Stan Sweetson, on the other hand, did *not* freeze. He just kept hauling ass.

Fusco appeared not to care. The cop stalked toward me. He had fired a warning shot in the air.

I wasn't sure if I should raise my hands. I decided against it when he holstered his gun. I glanced over at where Birch Sunday had been standing in a doorway.

No sign of him.

Fusco and I watched Sweetson's ungainly form flee into the tree line, disappearing from sight. Fusco's pale blue eyes, set in his flat face under the Smokey hat, shifted to me.

"Sorry about that, pal. Had to get your attention. What was up with you and that guy?"

"Excuse me, Officer Fusco, but am I under arrest?"

"Not yet, you ain't. You're being hauled in for questioning."

"Questioning? About what?"

"Murder." He nodded in the direction of his cruiser. "Let's go."

Chapter Twelve

Fusco suggested I ride up front with him as opposed to sitting in the backseat behind the wire mesh. It could have been a friendly gesture, allowing me "ride along" status. He must have figured that gave him a better chance at probing me with a question or two along the way. He left the siren off but used the rooftop lights. He clocked eighty miles per on the straightaway to Bisbee.

After a mile or two he said, "What was that about at the Ranch?"

There was no reason to dodge that one.

"I was looking for Janine Richards, the girl I was giving a lift to yesterday."

"I know who she is. You working for the family?"

He knew? Yesterday he seemed not to know . . .

"Something like that."

"So, what did they hire you to do? Funny stuff going on over at that cult, I'll bet, huh?"

I said, "Care to tell me where you're taking me?"

"You'll find out soon enough."

"Okay. Care to tell me *why* you're taking me there?"

"You'll find that out too. It's not my case. I'm running a favor for the County Sheriff."

"But it's not your case."

That shut him down from doing any more digging. We rode the rest of the way in silence.

This could only concern the Richards case. Either Janine or her mom. When we reached the traffic circle just below the Lavender Pit Mine, Fusco caught Highway 80 south and I knew it had to be Marna.

A building tightness began to curl my gut.

Marna . . .

I caught my first glimpse of the congestion of official vehicles clustered around her tipi and my throat constricted and went dry.

Fusco turned into The Tipi Lodge and parked as close as he could get to the scene.

It was a busy scene. County Sheriff vehicles, four of them. An ambulance. A police line had been marked and Marna's unit secured. A half-dozen or so uniformed cops were on hand, conducting activities in and around the area. The crackle and chatter of police band radios filled the sunny air. On the periphery the rubber-neckers hugged the police line; the ones always drawn to the scene of a tragedy like flies to a shithouse.

Janine and Del Richards sat in the Humvee, parked off to the side. They had to see Fusco escort me toward the tipi. There was no reason I saw to let on that I noticed them. From the corner of my eye, I could see that Janine held the scruffy little black mutt, Beauregard.

I followed Fusco into the tipi.

They'd covered her body with a plastic sheet. She lay stretched out on her back, half in and half out of the bathroom.

The man in charge was named Rivas. Tall, broad shouldered, in pressed khaki. Fusco introduced us and then faded into the background after a nod of thanks from the County man, who asked to see my credentials. Rivas's Latino features suggested a Native American strain in his DNA. He had cop eyes that missed nothing.

He returned my credentials and said, "Her husband was just in here and identified the body."

"I saw him outside with his daughter."

Rivas nodded.

"I told them to stand by. I'm not done with him. There's more to ask about. His contact info was on her phone. So we called him. He picked up his daughter on his way over. I haven't talked to her yet. He says his ex-wife hired you. So here you are."

He bent over and flicked back the sheet.

Marna wore a shapeless house robe. Nothing fancy or sexy, just something to lounge around in at the end of the day. One of her legs was bent under the other. Her arms were curved up, hands with the palms out. Her coloration was already like marble; a rictus of surprise and pain. Eyes wide. Mouth frozen in an oval.

I stood in the doorway for a better look at a cramped bathroom. Toilet tank cluttered with shampoo bottles. A shower stall with three kinds of soap in a wire tray hanging off the faucet. A nearby sink with a rusty vanity, door long gone. Perfume. Hand lotion. Toothbrush and toothpaste.

Blood smear on one corner of the sink.

Rivas said, "Because the units aren't connected, it wasn't until people started stirring this morning that they heard her little dog yowling. Someone notified the front office and the manager used his key and came in and found the body."

"So we don't know the exact time of death?"

"Not yet. Sometime around midnight is the head paramedic's best guess based on the condition of the body, but the M.E. will have to verify that. It's what we're working with now, though. She walked up to the convenience store behind this place last night at 11:30 for a bag of chips. The clerk's recollection was backed up by the register receipt we found in her purse. So peg it between midnight and two a.m. Of course, the medical examiner could find it was an accident. That she slipped and sustained a fatal blow to the back of her head on that sink." He let a significant pause draw itself out between us. "You do realize I'm extending you a professional courtesy by disclosing this information to you."

"I realize that. And you expect something in return."

He nodded.

"The State guys are on their way as we speak. I'd like to have something for them when they get here. So . . . the deceased hired you."

I said, "She retained the agency I work for." I gave him a business card. "The Honeycutt Agency assigned me to the case. So like you said, here I am."

"Why did she hire your agency?"

"She had concerns about her daughter. Janine belongs to that cult over in Gila Springs."

He frowned.

"Birch Sunday."

"That's the one."

"What have you dug up so far?"

"Nothing substantial. Janine's a good kid. Rebellious. Headstrong. But a nice kid."

"What about the ex-husband?"

"I was going to ask you about that. How did Richards react when he was brought in here?"

"No expression. Could have been shock."

"Or guilt. Care to make a call?"

"On her ex-husband? No, not yet. This early everyone involved is an unknown quantity."

"Suspect or person of interest?"

"It hasn't been determined yet if this is a homicide. She could have taken a tumble during the night. It happens. Half asleep. In the dark. First night in a new room. Call of nature. Maybe she tripped over her little dog."

I said, "Yeah, it could have happened that way."

"But you don't think so. You think it's foul play?"

I shrugged.

"I'm like you. Listening and paying attention."

"Uh huh. And when you do get around to drawing conclusions, you'll be sure to let me know, won't you?"

"Of course, I will."

I wasn't kidding, either. It's only in Hollywood fantasyland that the cops stand around in a homicide investigation while civilians, even if they're licensed, go about solving the crime. Doesn't work that way. If you're in my line of work, you keep the lines of communication with the authorities open and amicable.

Rivas said, "Okay then, we're done here. You need to stay in touch, McShan." He handed me one of his business cards. "I'm serious about that. Anything you come across that I should know, you make sure that I know about it."

I slid the card into my wallet.

"Can I have a second?"

"Make it fast," he said, "and don't disturb anything."

He left me alone with the body.

I knelt on one knee and eased back the sheet so I could gaze down at Marna one last time. I closed her eyes.

The spirit that had once inhabited these remains had traveled through the South spreading a mother's ashes. Could make a New Year resolution stretch into the monsoon season. Adopted a funny little dog off the street because it needed a home and she needed a friend.

I brushed a strand of her blonde hair back into place.

I said, "I'll find who did this, Marna. I promise."

When I stepped from the unit, Rivas was leading Del Richards in.

Richards pointedly avoided making eye contact with me.

Janine stood watching Beauregard frolic amid the high grass and weeds next to the Humvee. I walked toward them.

Janine and I had things to talk about.

Chapter Thirteen

Beauregard spotted me when I was fifteen feet away.

He immediately forgot about whatever he'd been so intently sniffing in the weeds. He forgot about Janine. He scurried in my direction, an unkempt charcoal blur beaming another of those silly doggie smiles, the tongue wagging from the side of his mouth. He raced up to me and rolled onto his back, legs waving excitedly in the air, begging for a tummy rub.

I leaned over and accommodated.

A jolt of sudden sadness washed through me. Marna had possessed a spirit that had reached out and touched me. How many others had been blessed to know that spirit along the way? Gone from the world forever. So damn sad. I buried the thought. This was no time to contemplate the sadness of our world. It was time to do something about it.

Janine came over to greet me. Still a pretty teenage girl from a distance but, up close, you could see a haunted expression. Tense and dark.

She said, "Did they let you see her?"

The flat tone matched her expression.

I nodded.

"I'm sorry, Janine. How are you doing?"

A shrug as only a teenager can shrug. Her eyes were on the doorway of her mom's tipi.

"I don't know. My dad came out to the commune to tell me. They want to talk to me but they won't let me see her body."

"You don't want to. Remember her the way she was."

"That should be easy," she said with another of those shrugs. "I was here to see her last night."

"Is that right?"

"I was upset. Stan Sweetson drove me here from the Ranch. He didn't want to, but I made him. I was wound up. Real upset."

"What about?"

"It doesn't matter."

"It did last night. It will matter to the police today. It matters to me."

At our feet, Beauregard scampered about excitedly from one of us to the other. Janine picked him up in her arms and held him close. The little guy nestled right in, happy to be safe.

Janine said, "What do they say happened? No one's told me anything. All I know is that Mom is dead. Shit. I should have gone with her on that trip to scatter Grandma's ashes. Shit."

"Tell me about your visit here last night."

"I had to see her. We talked."

"Did you call ahead and tell her you were coming?"

"No."

"How did she feel about that?"

"She was surprised. But she was glad to see me. We hugged. We cried."

"What did you talk about?"

She averted her eyes.

"Things. We hadn't seen each other in a while."

"And she didn't know you were coming to see her?"

""No. I told you. I was upset."

"And she was alive when you left?"

She blinked.

"Of course she was. What are you saying? You mean . . . do you mean that you think I . . . that I killed her?"

"Relax. No one says anyone killed her . . . yet. It could have been an accident. But let's say someone did murder your mother. The police are going to want to determine who did it. I just saw Stan before coming here."

"What about? What did he say?"

"Not much." I told her what happened when Fusco showed up in his cruiser. I said, "Now I'm more curious than ever about why Stan took off running. What happened last night after you saw your mother?"

"Nothing. Stan drove us back to the ranch. We said good night. End of story, believe it or not."

"Could he have doubled back on his own after he dropped you off?"

"I don't know. I guess he could have. But why would he?"

"I don't know," I said, shaking my head, "but here's what I do know. I made a promise to your mother just now, and I'll make the same pledge to you, Janine. If your mother did die by someone's hand, I will find that person and they will pay."

She looked sincere for once.

"I believe you."

"Okay then. If you believe me, tell me what you and your mom talked about last night?"

Her haunted eyes appraised me, then dropped.

"I can't. I . . . I can't—" She blinked, and I thought I saw a tear. She said, "Birch says that when we die, we're not transported to some perfect Heaven imagined by the theologians. Nor do we journey into the Unknown. We're going home. We return to our source. What do you think, Mr. McShan?"

I said, "I think it's time for me to get to work."

"Okay."

We traded a brief, chaste hug with Beauregard between us. I thought I heard the little mutt purring like a kitten.

I went about looking for Fusco's black and white but in vain. Officer Fusco was gone, most likely returned to his own jurisdiction after having delivered me here, stranding me at The Tipi Lodge without transportation. My Jeep Wrangler was at Birch Sunday's Spirit Ranch.

Janine and her father would be detained for at least a couple more hours, especially after Rivas got wind of Janine paying a visit to her mother last night. Much as I might have gleaned by hitching a ride back to the Ranch with them in Del Richards's Humvee, there was no way I was going to get stalled out waiting for them. If anything, their questioning would only extend once the State crime team arrived.

I drew out and checked my trusty, despised cell

phone. Three calls in voice mail from Agatha. I wasn't ready for that. I would call a local taxi service. That would get me a ride to the Jeep and—

That train of thought got derailed.

A snappy little red Corvette left the highway, turning into the busy, crowded parking lot of The Tipi Lodge.

Sherry Richards's car.

Coasting in my direction.

Chapter Fourteen

S herry had herself one hell of a black eye.

 I got a good look at it when I leaned over for a look through the 'Vette's open side window. Her left eye was that ugly purple of a brand-new shiner. Not completely swollen shut but that only made it worse because it provided a glimpse of a glazed, bloodshot eyeball.

"Need a lift?"

Her voice was perky but sounded forced.

"Big time," I said.

I got in beside her. She slid her sunglasses back up the bridge of her nose, concealing the black eye. She wheeled the Corvette around. An up-tempo country song twanged softly from the car stereo.

An oversized white van was just turning in from the highway. The crime scene crew had arrived.

Del Richards emerged from the tipi unit, walking toward his Humvee where Janine stood nearby while Beauregard relieved himself onto one of the vehicle's

front tires. Del did a double take when he caught sight
of the red Corvette.

Sherry flipped him the time-honored middle-finger
salute. She didn't just flip him the bird. She invested it
with the full treatment of spitefully narrowed eyes
shooting daggers and with her mouth a thin, down-
turned gash of belligerent hostility. She floored the
accelerator and we bolted away from there, spewing a
dirt-and-gravel shower in our wake.

The 'Vette fishtailed briefly. Then the tires met the
blacktop, and we were gone.

I said, "Rough night?"

She maintained a moderate speed. Five miles over
the posted limit. Her knuckles were white around the
steering wheel. She inhaled deeply. Exhaled slowly.

She said, "I thought about driving back to Bisbee
last to see you night, but I couldn't drag you into my
domestic strife, so I just took it. After he was . . . done
with me, I was in no shape to go anywhere. The worst
part is beating me up makes him horny. He . . . uses me,
then he passes out. If he caught me trying to leave, he
might kill me." She gave her head a short shake, as if to
clear it. "I don't want to talk about it."

"Then let's talk about today without any white lies."

A sideways glance from her good eye.

"That's a hell of a thing to say. I'm not going to lie
about anything, and I haven't lied about anything."

"Great."

"So what was that about a white lie?"

"You told Del last night, in the parking lot, that I
asked to see you. That was a little white lie. *You* who
showed up at The Copper Queen looking for *me*."

"Well, can you blame me?" She raised a hand to indicate her shiner. "I was trying to avoid *this*. How about letting me off the hook on that one?"

"Okay. So tell me about today."

"I woke up to Del's phone ringing. I felt like I was fixing to die. I heard him take the call. He got real serious and business-like and before I know it, he's tearing through the house, throwing on his clothes and I could hear him calling Janine, telling her he was coming to pick her up, heard him tell her he'd been notified by the police." She made a face. "He didn't tell me. He told her. Then he was out of there like a bat out of hell. I kept asking him what was going on and he finally told me as he headed out the door. He said it happened at The Tipi Lodge. Everyone knows that place. It's hard to miss from the highway. Then he was gone, and I went about trying to make myself look and feel halfway decent. I look like hell, don't I? And remember, no white lies."

"You'll survive. You've got a mirror. Leave me out of it."

The thin line of her mouth crinkled into a grin.

"An honest man! Mister, I'm liking you more and more."

"Why do you think Del didn't want you along this morning when he drove off?"

"He never wanted me along. He only wanted eye candy on his arm and a body to use in bed. McShan, when I met the guy, I was a dumb-ass starlet, if you can call it that, who thought she'd found a sugar daddy but got in way over her head before she knew it. That's pretty shallow, isn't it? Shallow Sherry, that's me. Or that *was* me. I've grown. I've wised up. I'm trying to toughen up. Del never let me anywhere near his life with Marna and Janine. Holidays, vacations with his daughter. And what was I supposed to say? I get Vegas twice a year. Once on my birthday and once for New Year's Eve. Everything else was him and Janine. I was never invited. I got used to that part. It's everything else between us that's not worth a damn anymore."

"So you followed him this morning?"

"No, I didn't follow him. It took me awhile to get myself into shape. I thought about you. I knew you'd be there so I drove there looking for you." Another sideways glance. "McShan, I need someone like you who can help me get away from Del."

I said, "Let's talk about his ex."

"Marna," she said.

"Ever meet her?"

"No. Like I said, Del was real big on the compartmentalizing. How did she die?"

"Fell and hit the back of her head on the bathroom sink."

"And they think it was murder?"

"It's too soon to tell. Forensics. Postmortem. The guy running the investigation is friendly enough, so I think he'll share information with me. Homicide is definitely a possibility."

"Say it was murder. Who would you pin it on?"

"You want me to say Del. He goes away on a murder rap, and you're done with him for good."

She nodded.

"Yes, that would be nice. Who else is there?"

"Well, there's Janine. She went to visit her mother last night."

"Oh my God! That would be terrible if it was her own daughter who killed her."

"It's terrible no matter who did it."

"Of course it is," said Sherry. "I'm not insensitive. You were working for Marna. Did you like her?"

"I did."

"Well then I'm sorry if what I said came out wrong." Sherry sighed. "I don't know. A girl killing her own mother? I can't imagine it! I'm sure Janine didn't do it. I hope she'll be all right."

I paused, then nodded.

"I was hired to look out for Janine. I intend to continue doing that. Do you know a guy named Stan Sweetson?"

"No."

"How about Johnny the Barber?"

She frowned.

"I don't know him but I know who he is. Del's mentioned him from time to time."

"In what way?"

"I don't recall. Just in passing, I guess."

"You know, there is one other person the police may decide to consider as a person of interest."

"You're referring to me?"

"I am."

"Well, that's just crazy. Why would anyone suspect me of killing anyone?"

"How's this: you killed Marna in order to frame Del for her murder as a way of getting rid of him."

"That's just silly. If I killed anyone it would be Del, believe me, not some innocent woman. But I'm no killer, McShan. See this black eye? I'm a victim."

"Did Del and Marna ever discuss reconciliation?"

"Oh, hell no. That breakup was as final as final could be. No, that never happened. Hey, maybe I killed Marna to keep her from stealing back my abusive partner."

It was my turn to sigh.

"Yeah, it does sound goofy when you put it that way. Tell you the truth, I don't think you have much to worry about from the police."

"I hope you're right. Everything that's happened . . . McShan, I've about had enough of this place and these people."

"You and Del reside in L.A., right?"

"That's right."

"But he maintains a home in Arizona."

"It's the house where he and Marna raised Janine. There are photographs of Janine at every age hanging in every hallway."

"Del's a sharpie. He doesn't impress me as the sentimental type."

"You've got that right. Del Richards is the most unsentimental man I've ever known. That detached tough guy pose is what drew me in at first. It only got bad between us when I came to realize that it isn't a pose. He's an unfeeling son of a bitch. Oh, his feelings for his flesh and blood kid are real enough but everybody else can go hang."

"So, if it's not sentimental, he's held onto his property here for another reason. With a guy like that, the only other reason would be because he's in business and making money."

She grinned.

"You're not only a detective. You're a good detective. The home here is a tax write-off."

"So he has a business interest in Arizona."

Her head bobbed.

"Sunrise Mining & Exploration."

"Marna told me he's a treasure hunting enthusiast."

"He is. When he wasn't off doing things with Janine, he was traipsing around the desert with his damn equipment. Sometimes she'd accompany him."

"Birch Sunday told me there have been drone flyovers quartering his land. Know anything about that?"

"I sure don't. Like I said, I wasn't exactly kept around to assist Del with his business dealings. I was his way of letting off pressure from dealing with all that."

"How involved is he in the company?"

"Well, when we come to Arizona, he can usually be found in the office." She rattled off an address on Fry Boulevard, the main business strip in Sierra Vista. She said, "Where am I taking you, by the way?"

We were approaching the traffic circle.

"I'm looking for something that won't be at Del's office," I said. "Mining and Exploration. They have a warehouse or a garage somewhere to store equipment."

"They do. I've been there a few times. I mean, I waited outside in the Humvee while Del went to meet someone."

"Any idea who?"

"I think he said it was an assayer from New Mexico."

"Stan Sweetson," I said, "the guy I asked you about. Okay. I want a look at that warehouse."

Chapter Fifteen

The warehouse was set back off the highway, out of town in a small industrial park on the east end of Sierra Vista, beyond the hospital. An oversized Quonset hut unmarked except for an address painted across its double wide doors. A ten-foot-high metal mesh fence topped by concertina wire surrounded the property. A compact of indeterminate age and make sat parked just inside the closed gate. Time and the owner had been tough on the modest conveyance. No hubcaps and a badly faded paintjob.

Sherry braked the 'Vette to a stop outside the gate.

I said, "Recognize the wheels?"

"No."

"It's not Del or Janine. We know where they are. You wait here. I'll nose around."

She pouted. That's the only word for it.

"Sure, why not? 'Wait in the car, Sherry.' Just like Del."

I said, "You're not with Del. When I detect, I detect alone."

"I'm sorry, McShan. I know who I'm with. When I get stressed, I get snarky. What if Del shows up while you're in there detecting?"

"All the more reason for me to make quick work of this."

I started to get out of the car.

She reached across and touched my arm, arresting my withdrawal. She sat sideways in her bucket seat to face me.

"Wait a sec. There's something you need to know."

"There's plenty I need to know. What have you got?"

"It's about me and you."

"Oh."

"Listen. Fair warning. I'm an impetuous girl. What you see is what you get with Sherry. So I'm not sure if this is the right time or the right thing to say but, uh . . . I think I may have fallen in love with you."

"Uh oh."

"I know. It's weird because I've only known you for twenty-four hours."

"It doesn't usually take women that long," I said. "I must be slipping."

What the hell was I supposed to say?

She was a sweet person with a nice personality and very easy on the eyes, yes indeed. Once upon a time Cheryl Bostwick from Janesville had taken on Hollywood with the intention of becoming the next Miss Thang. When that fell through, a hustler with bucks had seemed to her to be the next best thing. Who knew how many black eyes it had taken for her to seek a desperate way out. Sherry had no way of knowing the effect Marna Richards had had on me, or the way I was feeling this soon after having gazed down into Marna's dead face. My last sight of Marna had affected me more than I wanted to admit.

Sherry said, "Don't make fun of me. It's just that I'm having a real rough time of it right now. And I've never known anyone like you."

"Maybe you're lucky."

"Stop it," she said. "You can help me break away from Del."

"That's no reason to fall in love with me. And if he did murder his ex-wife like you hope he did, you won't need my help. The law will take care of him for you."

"Darn it, don't make me sound like a coldhearted bitch. I'm damn well entitled to feel the way I do. My whole head hurts from the punch in the face that bastard gave me last night. I just want everyone to get what's coming to them, and that includes me. I deserve better. Far better."

"I'll bet that's true," I said. "Tell you what, Sherry. I'll get you out of this. You don't have to pretend to be falling in love with me."

I intended that to end the conversation. I eased out of her car and closed the door. But I think I heard her through the half-open passenger window.

It sounded like she said, "But I *have* fallen in love with you."

A small box with a button was mounted on a fence pole by the gate. I pressed the button and waited. Nothing happened. I pressed he button again. Nothing. I pressed the button a third time. I studied the padlock on the gate. Standard make. A cinch for one of the passkeys I carry. A parked car did not necessarily mean someone was inside.

Then one of the double doors opened slightly.

A scraggly head poked out, reminding me of a turtle warily poking its head out from its shell. Eyes squinted against the sunlight, peering from behind thick eyeglasses. When he saw me, a slouch-shouldered young man emerged and approached me.

I say young man. Let me refine that.

A teenager. Younger than Janine and, at that age, a year or three can make a big difference. Fifteen, maybe sixteen. Five-eight. Slender. T-shirt emblazoned with a comic book action hero I didn't recognize. Sports trunks with the University of Arizona logo. Sneakers with brilliant red laces. The eyes behind the Coke-bottle-thick glasses shone with an intelligence muted by self-consciousness. A severe case of acne flamed as red as his shoelaces.

"Yes, sir?"

I said, "I'm Jack Howard. I'm here to see Del Richards."

That woke him up. His posture straightened.

"Uh, sir. Mr. Richards isn't here. You should try at his office."

He started to reel off the office address of Sunrise Mining and Exploration.

Good. The kid was out of the information loop. He most likely was unaware that Del Richards and his daughter were presently engaged in a police interrogation south of Bisbee. Very good.

I said, "Del and I spoke just a little while ago. He said to meet him here. Said he was on his way."

The kid reached into his back pocket and produced a cell phone.

"I'll give him a call. Mr. Richards is real busy. I'm sure if something came up and—"

I motioned for him to hold off on making the call, and he did.

"What's your name, son?"

"Jared."

"Tell you what, Jared. This is working out best for me, if you want to know the truth. I'm sure Mr. Richards will be along any second now but, uh, heh-heh —" I gave my impression of a conspiratorial chuckle, "— well, this is the first time I've ever hired his outfit. You work for his company, I see."

He blinked several times.

"Uh, no, not really. My mom's the bookkeeper there. Mr. Richards pays me to sweep this place out and stuff. You know."

Better and better.

"Tell you what, Jared. I'm hiring Mr. Richards to do a survey by air of some properties I own. But just between you and me, I wouldn't mind checking things out here on my own before he shows up. Uh, can do?"

Jared's mom, whoever she was, had done a fine job of raising her boy. He responded promptly to the authority of an adult. On the other hand, maybe Mom should have cautioned him not to be so trusting . . .

He unlocked the gate.

I was in.

Jared said, "I'll just leave the gate unlocked since Mr. Richards is on his way. He won't mind."

The interior of the warehouse was dim at first after the blazing sunlight, but my eyesight adjusted in short order thanks to a bank of overhead fluorescents that shone down on a wide array of assorted and neatly stored equipment. An evaporative cooler chugged away in a far window, providing minimal relief from the heat.

Jared's delay in responding to my buzzing at the front gate was explained by the military video game frozen on a PC screen. The work area in front of the monitor was littered with stacked, well-thumbed gaming books. The kid apparently was allowed to show up here when he felt like it, tend to whatever minor tasks were assigned him, and then he could then log in for endless gaming on the computer. Either that or the gaming was his secret little pastime. Paradise!

What caught my attention—what I'd come looking for—sat on the cement floor in the center of the warehouse, looking like nothing so much as a medium-sized, modified kite.

I indicated it with a nod.

"Reckon this is what they'll be using to survey my land?"

Jared's demeanor brightened. He was relieved to steer my attention away from his game on the boss's PC. He responded with the animated enthusiasm of a tech geek.

"An unmanned aerial drone." He spoke with such pride, you'd think he himself had designed it. "The Border Patrol and the Army use 'em to track drug smugglers and illegals."

I said, "An unmanned drone can survey land for mineral deposits, eh?"

"It sure can. Its payload is a magnetic sensor connected to a relatively simple 16-megapixel camera. This sweet baby flies over a designated target area, snapping pictures of the ground."

"And that's all there is to it?"

"Well, no. Someone on the ground has to have previously taken soil samples that have been analyzed. Then, for the flyover, they string out a cable across the soil where the samplings indicate potential. The cable has electrodes spaced out every five meters that send electrical currents some ninety meters into the bedrock. The drone flies over at a low altitude and electrical currents detect faults in the earth that could contain minerals. The information from the drone and the electrodes are fed into a computer that produces a 3D image so that—"

I interrupted him before my eyes had a chance to glaze over,

"What about the landowner's permission? That's required, isn't it, for a flyover survey of private property?"

He gave me an exaggerated wink.

"So they say."

"I heard Sunrise has done some surveying over in Gila Springs."

Another wink.

"Could be gold in them thar hills."

"No kidding? Who's the ground man over there?"

"It changes from job to job. I think Mr. Richards sent out of state for an assayer on that one."

I nodded as if I was someone in the know.

"Stan Sweetson. If we're going to map that way, how many overflights does it take?"

He took a step back, smart enough to realize when he was getting in over his depth.

"Uh, sir, you'll have to take that up with Mr. Richards. I would like to work for him someday but all I really know is what I hear when they're talking shop and I'm waiting for my mom to get off work."

I gave him a wink.

"You still know more than I do about this here drone."

Jared beamed at the compliment.

"It makes a few passes to map the coordinates, at least. Whoever is picking up signals on the ground records the coordinates on a laptop and emails them to the office, I do know that much. I did that once for Mr. Richards on a job when someone didn't show up. It was way cool."

"They're looking for gold over in Gila Springs?"

"Uh, sir, I really shouldn't be talking about that. Mr. Richards, he can tell you everything you need to know." Jared started back toward the PC. "I'd better get things squared away before he gets here. I get so involved in talking, I lose track of the time."

"Tell you what, son. I think you're right about him getting delayed." I glanced at my watch. "Me, I'm working a tight schedule today. Looks like I'll have to reconnect with him at a later date."

Jared gave a sigh that sounded like relief.

"Well, I'll be sure to tell him you stopped by, Mr. —?"

Perfect. He'd already forgotten my name. My phony name.

I brought out a wallet. I placed two twenties and a ten in his hand.

"Look, Jared, let's just keep this little visit between you and me, what do you say? I'll get in touch with Mr. Richards on my own."

He looked from the money in his hand up to me and back to the money. His expression grew doubtful

"I sure hope I didn't—"

"You didn't do anything wrong, son. You've been a big help. But this little conversation is just between the two of us, okay? It never happened. I was never here."

He pocketed the money.

"Sounds good to me."

Chapter Sixteen

I took Sherry to lunch in Sierra Vista.

She chose a Chinese restaurant located a few blocks from the offices of Sunrise Mining and Development. She'd never been to the restaurant, but she'd heard it was good. Del didn't like Chinese. I do. The service, the food and the atmosphere suited me just fine. We chose a booth in the rear. It was the beginning of the lunch hour and they were doing a brisk business. The murmur of conversation, the clink of silverware from other tables and traditional Chinese music playing at a low volume provided an ambiance that caressed and soothed the senses.

Sierra Vista sprawls out from Fort Huachuca, the southernmost major military installation in the U.S. Population: forty-four thousand. For the past several decades, "S.V." has been the fastest growing per capita community in Arizona. Military personnel. Ex-military personnel. Civilian retirees. Snowbirds. The town provides every service imaginable, conveniently concentrated along two major thoroughfares serving not only local customers but also those from outlying communities like Benson, Tombstone, Bisbee, Douglas, and Agua Prieta, Mexico. Sierra Vista is a busy place but one of its charms is that you can drive fifteen minutes in any direction and be right back out in the wilderness.

I was ready for a respite from having spent the day thus far driving hither and yon, trying to discern who was lying and who was telling the truth.

I'd put my emotions on the back shelf of my mind. Work, not emotion, drove me. But I just couldn't seem to forget those brogans I'd seen on the front step of Marna's tipi. She thought she was safe. Don't we all? No one wakes up in the morning expecting it to be their last day. Expecting to be murdered.

Marna.

Poor Marna.

Sherry and I kept the conversation light. To be perfectly honest, it was difficult to dwell on sadness with Sherry at the table. Her shiner remained concealed behind those Hollywood sunglasses. She looked like a million bucks.

We got around to serious topics an hour later, near the end of the drive back to Spirit Ranch to reclaim my vehicle.

She said, "I'm going straight home after I drop you off. Del will have his hands full today between the cops and his office. I'll be gone by the time he gets home."

"Sounds prudent," I said.

She asked for my cell phone number, which I gave her. She steered us off the state highway, onto the gravel county road that led to the ranch.

"Thanks for lunch, McShan. You're good company.

These past twelve hours have been rough. You've been the only saving grace. And now for you it's back to work. Is any of this starting to make sense to you?"

"Some."

"I need to know," she said, "before anything else happens. Is Del involved?"

"He found out there's gold on Birch Sunday's land."

"Does Birch know?"

"About the gold? I'm not sure. I don't think so. I'm not even sure he cares. He's real attached to his land. He knows something is up. He complained to me about drone flyovers and that's exactly what Del has been up to. Your boyfriend is scheming to get that land."

"*Ex*-boyfriend as of last night. But can he legally acquire land that someone doesn't want to sell?"

"That's part of the puzzle. I doubt he's made an offer to Birch Sunday. Doesn't feel that way. The situation is fluid."

"What about Janine?"

"That's what I'm trying to find out," I said. "Did her dad get interested in that property after she joined their group? Did he nose around and find what he found maybe from old forgotten documents and records of the original mining company that owned the land? Birch has all the signs of a distant relative who inherited the property because the estate wanted to unload it. So Del is up to whatever he's up to and Janine's got nothing to do with it. Or are she and Dad in on it together? He found out about the gold deposit, which must be significant, and they placed her in the cult and Birch Sunday's inner circle so she can influence him and bend his will to sell out to her father."

"That would call for some influence."

"Clean her up some and Janine could influence most any man if she set her mind to it. I hope it doesn't break that way. I like her. Attitude to spare but everyone's got their reasons. I'd hate to find out she's a scheming little so-and-so."

"That's why Marna sent for you, isn't it?"

"I don't know what Marna knew but yeah, it's why I'm here. And with Marna gone, that girl needs my help more than before. If Marna was murdered, it ties in together."

Sherry winced at the 'Vette's shuddering shake and shimmy as we traveled the road at a crawl. The road was in fact well maintained. The only real affect was her sporty car acquiring a fresh coat of road dust.

There were more vehicles in the parking lot when we arrived than before. Guys were unloading guitar cases and electric amplifiers from a van. Some sort of outdoor performance was being set up. Additional vehicles had recently arrived. Folks were showing up with plates of food. A potluck dinner in the making with live entertainment.

Sherry braked to a stop next to my Jeep. I started to climb out of the 'Vette. Before I knew it, she had turned in her bucket seat and planted a kiss square on my lips. A warm, moist, tender kiss, accompanied by fingertips that delivered a brief caress about my left ear.

I hadn't expected that.

And I didn't mind it.

We parted without speaking. I watched her drive away.

What a day.

I checked my phone. Voice mail from Rivas, asking me to return his call. I did so.

He got right to it.

"Looks like homicide. We've only got the onsite prelim. In a case like this there'll be a complete autopsy scheduled. There were bruises under her clothing that indicate she was pushed or shoved in some sort of physical altercation and when she fell, she hit the back of her head on the sink at such an angle and with enough force for it to be a fatal blow."

"If it happened that way, there's still the question of premeditated or accidental."

He said, "Care to bet on which way a defense attorney would run with it if it gets to court?"

I said, "How are you going to run with it?"

"Ex-husbands are often suspect number one, especially with a guy like Del Richards. The guy's a hustler."

"You noticed."

"A lot of good it did me. The State guys are running the show now. Matter of fact, I'm out of the loop completely unless they tap me for local color. Jurisdictional bullshit."

"What's their thinking on it?"

"They're focusing on the girl. The daughter and some guy from the cult drove down to see the Richards woman sometime last night. A guy named Sweetson."

There was no reason to mention that I already knew about that. Rivas would want to know why I hadn't volunteered the information in the first place. I anticipated having enough trouble explaining and defending myself to Agatha. I didn't need an additional sideshow, having to explain and defend myself to the law. So I stayed mum about Sweetson. Given the natural confusion that occurs most times when there's multi-agency intersection, it was likely that Officer Fusco of Gila Springs was not privy to details of this investigation and so, not realizing the significance of Sweetson to the investigation, had not bothered to mention to Rivas the man he saw fleeing for the tree line at Spirit Ranch.

On the other hand, while Rivas hadn't given me anything the Honeycutt Agency couldn't have gotten a line on in a day or so, time was of the essence in a case like this and so, yeah, I owed him something.

I gave him the lowdown on Del Richards's company conducting flyovers of The Spirit Ranch with an unmanned drone. He heard me out.

"Thanks, McShan. I'll see that gets passed along."

"You said you're off the case."

"I'm still an interested observer with connections. But yeah, I'm on the sidelines now that State's handling the homicide."

"Sure you are," I said. "The sideline's the best place to keep a close eye on the action."

"I just don't like people getting murdered in my jurisdiction, is all."

"Rivas, I can help you clear this thing up. You can serve it up to them on a platter, the whole case."

Several seconds passed. He was processing that.

Then he said, "What else have you got?"

"I've got questions."

"Try me."

"Fusco. Gila Springs."

"I know who he is. Dumb but clean."

"Johnny the Barber."

I could practically hear a tight grin crease his face across the connection.

"You do get around. Watch that one. Johnny's too slick for us—so far. His own kind will take care of him. Him and that sister of his. Yolanda. Joined at the hip. She handles the dirty work. He's a pretty good barber from what I hear. Go on, McShan. Tell me you're going to take down Johnny the Barber for me."

"I'd only tell you that if I thought it was true. So the biker gal is his sister."

"Half-sister, if it matters. She's the one to watch. The word is she's committed three separate murders in Mexico in the past year and she got away with each one."

Chapter Seventeen

In what is called the Four Corners area—where the state lines of Colorado, Arizona, New Mexico and Utah intersect—Mesa Verde is a popular tourist attraction and national park. Home of the ancient Anasazi, it is the largest archeological preserve in North America. The Cliff Palace includes 600 cliff dwellings inhabited fifteen hundred years ago by a people who survived using a combination of hunting and gathering and the farming of crops such as corn, beans, and squash.

Today, all that remains are the stony ruins of their cave dwellings where once a mighty metropolis thrived. Drought and famine led to their abandonment of Mesa Verde. The Anasazi have since been lost to the mists of time. Put simply, after the water disappeared, so did they. They moved on. They found some better place to hunt their game and plant their crops. They found a place with water.

Some day, a century or three from now if there's anyone left on the planet, they're going to stand ruminating the same way about the fate of those who left behind places like Phoenix, Tucson, and Sierra Vista, where people settled because there was water. With an ever-expanding Sunbelt population and the urban landscape continuing to sprawl across the desert, you'd assume there was no reason to think it wouldn't last forever.

But it can't. The desert isn't made that way.

The water for the countless kitchen taps, showers and flushed toilets diminishes a water table that's artificially re-directed from somewhere else, thanks to modern technology. As long as technology and natural resources are sustainable, everything is on track. But one need only consider the pyramids of ancient Egypt or the cliff palace of the Anasazi to witness how the sands of time will ultimately level culture and civilization.

The urban communities that dot the arid Southwest today are the ruins of the future. There wasn't enough water to sustain their civilization, archaeologists of a distant future will say while they observe the faded grandeur of a world that once was. Why did they settle and build without sustainable resources? What were they thinking?

The offices of *Sunrise Mining and Exploration* in Sierra Vista shared a strip mall with a music shop, a dealer in rare coins, and an optometrist, not far from Fort Huachuca's main gate.

Sierra Vista had grown from a cavalry outpost of the 1870s, tasked with protecting settlers from murderous Apaches and Mexican banditos, into the thriving community of today. Fort Huachuca is home to the U.S. Army Intelligence Center and the 9th Army Signal Command, which handles front line communications in combat zones throughout the world. Those serving here are the high-tech, upper-echelon "white collar warriors". During a typical working day, twenty thousand people are on base and that makes for plenty of traffic along Sierra Vista's main drag, Fry Boulevard.

That traffic noise and activity is why Del Richards didn't spot me. I sat at the steering wheel of the Jeep Wrangler.

Also, as he left his office, he was occupied with something—someone—else.

A blonde number who looked to be a well-cared for thirty. Her height, frame and build could have been mistaken from a distance for either Marna or Sherry.

She accompanied Del from the office so they could be alone in the vestibule. I saw their figures merge for a brief embrace and a mouth-to-mouth kiss, visible from the street if anyone (like me) cared to watch but not within view of the young guys poring over a map inside the office, visible to me through a plate-glass window. The business name was printed in gold letters across the glass.

Del Richards and the woman broke their clinch in the vestibule. She stood in the doorway as he passed on his way out. She wore a blouse and skirt that were just a bit too tight for the office. She wore stiletto heels. Del let the palm of his hand brush across her accentuated and not unattractive butt. He sneered something in her ear that prompted a girlish blush. Then the door closed between them.

Through the plate-glass window, I saw her return to the office. The guys around the map looked up. She was worth a look. She started a conversation with them.

Richards sauntered across the parking lot toward his Humvee which happened to be next to my vehicle.

You encounter all sorts in my line of work and you have to withhold judgment on most of them and just do your job unless they've really stepped over the line. I had a strong negative gut reaction to this guy. It wasn't just that he was a swaggering misogynist and proud of it. I've encountered more than a few of those and in fact have partnered with a few in law enforcement. This huckster wore his primal, predatory meanness in the open like he was proud of it.

I stepped from the Jeep to meet him, wondering two things.

Was the woman, with whom he was obviously having a workplace affair, Jared's mother? And in her bad-mouthing of Del, Sherry had not bothered to include infidelity. Because she didn't know about the office romance? And those guys in Del's office. Were they gloating over a map of Birch Sunday's property? They reminded me of pirates poring over their swag.

Del saw me and glowered.

"What the fuck are you doing here? If you're looking for my kid, I dropped her off at the ranch."

"I'm looking for you, Del. We need to talk."

"About what? I saw you out there this morning where Marna died. She hired you but now she's dead. End of story. End of you."

"Sounds like someone doesn't want me around."

"Say, you are sharp."

"Is it because you've got something to hide, Del?"

"Fuck you, McShan. You and the cops think that I killed Marna, don't you? Well, I didn't."

"What does your daughter think?"

"My daughter is not your business. You heard me. You were hired. Now you're fired. Get lost. Case closed."

"Maybe, maybe not. Let's you and me talk about Stan Sweetson."

"Who? What the hell kind of name is that?"

I said, "You want Birch Sunday's land. You imported an assayer from out of state to help you and keep the lid on what you're up to. His cover was to join Birch Sunday's group. He assisted you in an aerial survey of The Spirit Ranch. Sweetson took off but your daughter is still in place."

"You leave my daughter out of this."

I said, "No, I'm not about to do that. Janine is why I'm here."

"I'm her father, damn you. It's my job to look out for her."

"She can do better. Birch told me he'll never sell his land. He's the idealistic type. You're working around that. Your daughter is a trusted member of his inner circle. I even caught a romantic vibe between the two of them. Is that according to plan?"

He considered me.

"Y'know, McShan, I could play this by the rules and take out a restraining order against you. You're hassling me at my place of business. I haven't done anything wrong."

I said, "At first,

I thought your daughter and Stan Sweetson were honeys. But I was wrong. Maybe she's your eyes and ears over there at the ranch. Is she there to angle Birch into a relationship, into bed? Make him pliable, then you move in."

"You're talking trash, McShan. You don't know shit."

"I know what I've seen with my own eyes."

His eyes became chips of ice.

"Now what are you talking about?"

"I saw Stan Sweetson and Janine quarreling at lunch yesterday. If it wasn't a lover's quarrel, what were they arguing about? If Stan Sweetson went to Birch Sunday and blew the whistle on you, Birch would see to it one way or another that you never, ever got his land. Stan Sweetson was threatening to spill to Birch Sunday your whole deal and he has some sort of documentation to back it up. He was showing that to Janine when he made his pitch at the Dos Pesos. He must have been afraid of you so he made the pitch through your kid. How am I doing?"

"Piss poor. Everything you're throwing at me is pure conjecture."

"But you're not denying it, are you, Del? That's the only way it plays. Poor Sweetson. Even after all that, when Janine got desperate to see her mom last night she hit Stan boy up for a ride. But then you know that."

"The cops told me about it. So what?"

I said, "I saw Sweetson this morning. He was scared to death and literally running for the hills. What I'm wondering is, did you just throw a scare into him . . . or did you call in Johnny the Barber and his sister to drop the hammer as an object lesson to anyone else who might get a stupid idea like crossing you? I'm going to find out. If you had Sweetson capped, you're going down for it."

The son of a bitch actually gave me a cocky wink.

"You're on. In the meantime, McShan, stay away from me . . . and stay away from my daughter."

He stepped past me, climbed into his ostentatious gas guzzler and steered the Humvee out of the parking lot, accelerating and loudly merging with the traffic flow along Fry.

Chapter Eighteen

I called Agatha while driving down Highway 92 on my way back to Gila Springs. She knew who it was from her caller ID.

"McShan, I told you the last time we spoke that I expect promptness in all communications between you and this office."

"Expect away. Things are happening in Arizona."

"Such as?"

"We've lost a client."

"What do you mean, 'lost a client'? I told you last time this happened that if you alienated one more customer and drove away business, McShan, I'd—"

"Marna Richards is dead."

She didn't so much as draw a deep breath or sigh.

"Oh. Report."

I ran through the timeline since our last conversation. Agatha was a good listener when she wanted to be. I kept it brief.

When I was done, she said, *"So then you know all about Stanley Sweetson. And you don't need to know anything about Johnny the Barber since you're all done down there in Arizona."*

"Hold on. Yeah, I know Sweetson. But he's gone missing. He's a person of interest in the murder investigation even if the cops don't know it yet. Tell me about Johnny the Barber."

She said, *"He's good at staying one step ahead of the heat. Busted as a teenager. A hot car ring out of Agua Prieta. The judge gave him a chance to enlist to avoid prison and he took it, but they ended up kicking his ass out of the Army two years later. Says here honorable discharge but that's because at the time the Army wanted to downplay drug use in the ranks, so they just quietly swept guys like Johnny out the door. But wait a minute. McShan, you do not need this information and you know why. You're out of there."*

"Agatha. Two words. Murder investigation."

"Uh huh. I'm sure you came clean with the authorities like you're supposed to. You are done, McShan. The client is dead. The account is closed."

"Not for me it's not. This is more than a case. This is a person. Her name is Janine. She's the client's daughter and I was brought in to straighten out any trouble she's in. That account is open until that job is done."

"Now you listen to me, young man. I'm running a business here, not a charity. This old world is full of people in trouble. People in need. Believe me, running Daddy's agency has made me all too aware of that. But I didn't turn this agency around into a paying proposition by being a bleeding-heart humanitarian like Daddy was. I've got paying customers lined up in Dallas, Atlanta and one all the way up there in Fargo. I'm way short on

human resources and that's something I don't like. So don't make yourself part of my problem!"

"Agatha, do you think I don't understand business?"

"Sure seems that way, the way you're going on."

"Listen to me. Say I hand this over to the sheriff's office down here with a gift-wrapped solution to the Marna Richards's murder, courtesy of Honeycutt Personal Services. You can't pay for publicity like that."

"I see where you're heading with this and I don't like it."

"Boss, here's the deal. I'm not leaving Arizona until I straighten out Janine Richards's life one way or another. That girl needs my help and she's going to get it, whether she likes it or not."

A long pause. Then:

"McShan, do you know why I sometimes give in when you and I butt heads like this?"

"I like to think it's because of my good looks and power of persuasion."

"It's not. You remind me of my father. Until I met you, my daddy was the most cocksure, bullheaded man I ever did know."

"Uh, thanks, I think."

"Let me finish. And Daddy, God love him . . . he was always right."

This time she was the one who terminated the connection.

Chapter Nineteen

Today the monsoon would deliver.

The clear blue sky was yielding to low cloud cover encroaching from the south. You could smell rain on the heavy air. Thunderheads were piling up in the distance. Lightning was beginning to dance and leap. Wicked, jagged slashes of bright silver speared through the clouds, tailed by thunder that sounded like the booming of artillery in the distance.

Yolanda should have been roasting in the tight black leathers that encased her Amazonian proportions, but she gave no sign of discomfort, kneeling there and working at something on her Harley, exactly as she had on my visit the day before. She looked cool and sleek, her luxurious hair collected at the nape of her neck. Another repeat of my previous visit: she made no acknowledgment of my presence when I walked past her.

Johnny, bathed in sunlight through the shop's plate-glass window, had surely noted my approach. When I stepped inside, he continued perusing his newspaper for the time it took him to finish reading whatever article had him so engrossed. A performance for my benefit. When he pretended to notice me for the first time, he folded the newspaper and set it aside. He remained seated, legs nonchalantly crossed at the knees.

"Late in the day for a shave, amigo."

"No shave," I said. "Information."

The briefest smile.

"Ah, the return of Don Quixote."

"Yesterday you said that you didn't know Del Richards. I've since learned that was a lie . . . amigo."

A mild, distinctly Latin shrug.

"It is necessary for you to understand, amigo, that discretion and confidentiality between a man and his barber is as sacrosanct as that between doctor and patient or priest and confessor. Surely you appreciate this, no? Your questions yesterday placed me in an awkward position."

In the mirror, I watched Yolanda position herself in the doorway like yesterday.

I said to Johnny, "Are you in Del's pocket?"

"Hardly that." He scrutinized his manicured fingernails with mild, distracted satisfaction. "On occasion I perform odd jobs for Señor Richards."

I said, "I can imagine one of those odd jobs. We're just up the road from The Spirit Ranch. Janine Richards favors Dos Pesos next door for lunch. You're perfectly positioned to keep an eye on her for her father."

Johnny said, "Maybe so."

"And your sister here coming to Janine's rescue yesterday, taking on those *cholos*. The girl missed it but not me. You and Yolanda operate on a small turf, and you don't draw attention to yourselves, especially with Officer Fusco sitting across the highway observing like he was yesterday, unless you're being paid. You had no choice but to send Yolanda in when those boys started acting up. How about Fusco? Is he on the payroll?"

"Windmills, Don Quixote. Windmills."

"I'm sure you've heard what happened to Marna Richards."

"I had nothing to do with that. Nothing."

"What about Stan Sweetson?"

He rose from the barber chair. He positioned himself behind it, so it was between us.

He said, "Sweetson. I don't know that name."

"That's no answer. That's what you said about Del Richards yesterday." I made eye contact with Yolanda's reflection in the mirror. "What about you, big girl? I heard about those homicides they can't pin on you down in Mexico. Maybe Sweetson was your first kill north of the line."

Yolanda said to her brother, "Juan, this one is big trouble. You said I could have him."

I spoke to Johnny but kept an eye on Yolanda.

"Is that what you told her? That's no way to be. Sweetson put the squeeze on Del, who pays the two of you to take care of little problems like that."

"I told you, amigo—"

"Yeah, right. You never heard of Sweetson. So what?" I indicated Yolanda. "That's why you keep her around."

Yolanda left her position in the doorway and eased toward me with the fluidity and economy of movement of a dangerous jungle cat. Everything about her said trouble.

I didn't have much choice but to let her make the first move. I can read people, sure. But I could have been mistaken about her intention and I didn't want to pop this big honey only to find out that all she wanted was to be loud and make faces. I was ready for anything . . . except what happened next.

Her left hand shot forward and snapped shut. A tightening grip around my scrotum, through the fabric of my slacks. We stood toe to toe. Her eyes maybe five inches from mine. She was taller than I am. The tremble of a depraved smile quirked her lips.

She said, "If you live after this, *cabron*, you'll never be good for a woman again."

I spoke to Johnny over her shoulder.

"Tell her to back off."

Johnny said nothing. He merely gave his head the slightest shake, no. He wore an amused smile, and I knew why. If I let Yolanda push me around, I'm bested by a woman and word gets around. Words like "laughing stock". On the other hand, if I take her down, word gets around just as fast that big bad McShan has clobbered a woman. There was no way I would walk away from this in good standing.

Because these two were enjoying themselves so damn much, the tableau held like that for a few seconds —me trying to maintain a minimal degree of decorum while a hulking lesbian biker bitch held my nuts like a vise and all but laughed in my face.

I wasn't looking forward to this.

Yeah, she was big and tough. But I would let her find out for herself what trouble was.

I gave her a swift kick. The toe of my boot caught her in the shin. She howled her pain, her grip reflexively releasing my scrotum. I threw a straight right that caught her inches above her belt buckle, making her grunt. She staggered back, regaining her balance, sucking air into her lungs. Her blazing eyes were half-veiled now. I've never seen such menace in a woman's face.

Johnny said in a quiet voice, "Finish him off."

I concentrated, waiting for her to move. I sidled, preventing her from trapping me against the wall. She came in with surprising speed. She threw a right at my face. I dodged out of its path. I swung my right into her midsection. Yolanda roared like a stung mama lion. She swung and damn if she didn't catch me on the side of the head with a ham-sized fist. Lights started flashing and bells started ringing inside my head. Her oversized fist found an opening and landed again. And double damn if I didn't feel the floor slope upward and slam me in the face.

Johnny said, "Stomp him."

She reached down and caught me by the shoulder. She rolled me onto my back. I gave thought to resisting. Reality was out of focus. Spinning around me. I couldn't seem to get a grip on it. Above me, Yolanda grinned. She licked her full, ruby lips expectantly. She raised her heavy boot.

I forced air into my lungs. I shook my head to dispel the fog. No one wins every brawl, and over the years I've taken my lumps—granted, not from Amazonian Latinas in black leather—but I'm hard to kill. This was not my day to die. I caught her foot and twisted. I shoved with all my strength.

Yolanda flew backwards, landing on the customer chairs and shattering them beneath her. I struggled to my feet. Snarling, she pulled herself out of the wreckage of the chairs.

I backpedaled, leaving it to her to decide what would come next. Old School was fouling me up again. Bottom line was I'm a boy and she's a girl and is it right for boys to fight with girls? I wasn't raised that way.

She threw caution to the wind. She rushed me. Screeching like a banshee. Going for my throat. What the hell. I sidestepped and buried my right fist to the wrist in her midsection. It doubled her over. I brought up my knee and it caught her in the face. There was a crunching sound as her nose broke. I chopped down at the base of her neck with the side of my hand in a rabbit punch. She hit the floor face first and didn't move, snorting bubbles of blood from her shattered nose.

I turned to see what Johnny was up to.

He had just started coming at me with a straight-edge razor. Deadly squint with the arm drawn back for a swipe at my jugular. But he'd hesitated a few heart-beats too many before dealing himself in.

I said, "Don't."

Maybe it was the edge in my voice or the squint set to my eye. Could have been the sight of his sister, prop-ping herself up in the corner, the lower half of her face covered with flowing blood. Whatever it was, Johnny drew up short, holding eye contact with me. Then he lowered his arm and set the straightedge razor on the counter under the mirror.

I said, "Sweetson. What did you do with him?"

"We didn't kill him, I can tell you that. Yolanda paid him a visit late last night. She recommended that he be gone by first light."

I said, "He was a little behind schedule when I saw him, but he was on his way."

"We only scare him. With Yolanda, that is enough."

"I'll buy that. She is a scary one. Okay, prove it."

"Prove it?"

"You're an operator, Johnny. A two-bit border rat but you're slick enough to cover your ass in case of emergency. In case anything goes wrong. Well, something went wrong. A woman was murdered last night. Now I'm supposing, to cover your ass you've got a contact number, maybe more than one, for Stanley Sweetson. Okay. So, get him on the phone." I brought out my cell phone. "What's his number? When he and I talk, then I'll know he's alive."

He referred to his cell phone directory and called off a number.

Nobody said anything while I let the number ring.

A perky male voice came on: *"Hi. This is Stan. Your call is important to me. Please leave your name, number and a brief message."*

Perky. Very much alive.

I said, "Stanley, this is McShan. We had a brief encounter this morning before you took off running from The Spirit Ranch. You need to call me. There's been a homicide. This is no damn joke. Call me and we'll straighten it out."

I pocketed the phone.

Johnny said, "He's alive. He'll call you."

I said, "No wonder he was skittish when I saw him this morning. He drove Janine Richards to Bisbee to see her mother before the murder last night and then he gets a visit from Yolanda. He had a busy night. Maybe he doesn't even know there's been a murder . . . unless he's the one who did it."

"I will see that he calls you. I tell you, we did not kill him."

Johnny squeezed between me and the counter to crouch beside his sister. He grabbed some tissue and tried to dab at her injured nose. Yolanda brushed his hand away irritably. Dark eyes, burning with fury, glared up at me.

I turned to Johnny.

"You know what, amigo? I believe you. You've got yourselves a good thing going here, moving hot cars, bringing in dope and illegals. Keep a short leash on your sister and you've got a bright future in the world of criminal enterprise. You're too smart to fuck that up with a murder."

He started to say something.

Yolanda strong-armed her brother aside with a backhand forceful enough to send Johnny toppling into the broken-up customer chairs. Then she sprung at me like an oversized jack-in-the-box, a ham-like fist scooping up the straightedge razor from the counter. She came at me with the razor flashing and slashing.

Oh, man!

She dropped on me with the full-throated shriek of a warrior goddess. A towering, hulking human tornado, damn straight. As for me, I don't know where our strength comes from at a time like that. I'm five-ten, weighing in at one-eighty, so I'm no featherweight. I twisted away from her, showing her my back. I stooped down so her momentum pinned her bulk to my back, and I put that moment to use, turning her size and weight against her. Getting the right grip on her, in one smooth, continuous motion I fulcrumed her over my shoulders under the force of her own forward momentum and sent the big girl flying, upside down, through the doorway of the barbershop, into her motorcycle, creating one hell of a racket when her heft knocked the bike over by toppling into it, entangling her beneath it.

Johnny was picking himself up inside the shop. Dusting himself off. His dazed expression said he wasn't sure what to expect next, and who could blame him?

When I stepped past Yolanda on my way out, she was sitting up with the Harley-Davidson pinning her down at the knees. She held her head in both hands. She looked like an ox smacked across the head with a sledgehammer.

I made it to the Jeep and drove away without taking my eyes off her in the rearview mirror.

Just in case.

Damn!

Chapter Twenty

Tumbleweeds danced across the county road, the motion so fluid as to seem choreographed. Restless Mother Nature scrambled the clouds darkening by the minute, scudding overhead, lowering the ceiling of visibility until the sky seemed to boil with turbulence. The rumble of thunder reverberated through the air, so loud, as it drew closer, the temperature plummeting. Gusts of wind, moist with the scent of rain, ruffled wildly weaving tree limbs.

My head was starting to clear from the punches landed by the mighty Yolanda.

Marna Richards had been right about her daughter being involved in something over her head. I still hadn't determined the precise nature of Janine's involvement in her father's land scheme. Was it voluntary, resulting in her placement as her father's secret operative in Birch Sunday's group? Or had her involvement in the group come first, and then been exploited by her father? Once I knew the answer to that question, I'd know what to do.

It had become a complicated case considering the short time since I'd arrived and the small circle of people involved.

Del Richards had learned about the gold deposits on Birch Sunday's property. How that came to be didn't matter much at this late date. He brought in the out-of-state guy, Sweetson, to assist him in verifying that yes, there was indeed gold in the ground beneath The Spirit Ranch. Enough gold to make it worth finagling for.

Birch Sunday. A man of deep personal convictions with strong emotional ties to his land. He has no intention of selling. So Del is working what angles he can to get the land. Sweetson saw a chance to shake him down, threatening to expose him to Birch. Stan made his pitch through Janine, but that whole deal went south—or rather, east back to Albuquerque—after Stan received a late-night visit from Yolanda.

I wondered how much, if anything, Janine knew about any of this.

So . . . okay. Sure. Except for the little matter of why I'd been hired—to straighten out Janine's troubled teenage life—everything else on that side of the equation seemed to fit.

That left the murder of our client.

Who killed Marna Richards?

If I let Johnny the Barber and his homicidal nut sister off the hook, that left me with five suspects: Del Richards and his daughter, Janine. Stan Sweetson. Del's live-in girlfriend, Sherry. And Birch Sunday. To an extent Del and Sherry canceled each other out because they'd been together last night, locked in domestic conflict. I couldn't imagine a motive for Birch Sunday to kill Marna but he was mixed up in this because it was his land, so he remained a maybe on the suspect list. As for Johnny and Yolanda . . . were they really off the hook? They did handle Del Richards's dirty work.

My only course was to work with what I had, which was Time and Suspects. The time had been set by Agatha and the only suspect I didn't have access to was Stan Sweetson. As for Del, Janine and Birch, it was time to go to work eliminating them one at a time until a "last suspect standing" would point me to the answer.

The gravel parking lot at the Ranch was full to capacity when I got there. Every make, model and class of vehicle imaginable. New and old. Pickups, SUVs, beat-up economy cars and a handful of motorcycles. A medium-size crowd of maybe seventy or eighty folks, gathered around amplifiers and a drum set where a rock band played. Not earsplitting punk rock or heavy metal, thank God. What I heard when I stepped from the Wrangler sounded like a pleasant enough medium tempo Grateful Dead jam.

The low clouds began misting with a light sprinkling of rain drops. Considering the muggy heat of the day, it was a welcome relief. Heavy, darker clouds and lightning continued to close in from the south.

Folks were pointing, urging each other to view the sky behind me. I cast a glance in that direction. A rainbow, enormous and perfectly articulated, arced magnificently against a scant patch of blue sky to the north. Missing was beer and alcohol. Plenty of water bottles and soda. Blankets had been spread out. Coolers looking like shiny tombstones for the thirsty. Rickety lawn chairs. A few longhairs—guys and gals—gyrated languidly to the music in front of the band. Children and dogs wandered freely. The spectrum of age, dress and grooming choices were as wide as the range of vehicles in the parking lot.

Rural life is an egalitarian proposition. In the city, "tribal" defines the nightlife. This is an urban dance club. That's a country western bar. This is a punk rock hangout. That's a biker dive. And of course, the gay and lesbian bars and discos. But it's different out in rural communities and small towns in the boonies where the social venues are far more limited. Chances are bikers and cowboys and soldiers and gays and students will all patronize the same bar or two that exist in these communities.

This was reflected in the makeup of the crowd.

No sign of Birch Sunday or Janine.

I heard myself being hailed with a friendly greeting by Larry and Linda, the middle-aged couple with whom I'd had a friendly conversation at the service the previous day. Like everyone else, Larry and Linda glowed with a sunny disposition despite the bleak weather.

We chatted idly for a few minutes as people do. They were here to visit with their friends. They gestured broadly to the other attendees. Nice, gracious people. I managed to work in a reference to Birch, saying that I had expected to see him here.

The consensus was that they too were surprised at his absence. Birch had driven into Sierra Vista that afternoon, they'd heard. It was assumed that he had been delayed and would arrive soon. He'd gone to pick up some gardening supplies at the Super Walmart.

That in itself could have explained his delay. In these parts, Walmart is as much a social hub as a mecca of consumerism. In cities, where folks have access to all manner of large and small shops and stores for their every want and need, places like Walmart are held in disdain. Denigrated with the term "box store". But they're practical places for people to meet in small-town rural communities. Kind of a super convenience store. You can make a quick one-stop and pick up a new shirt, a frozen chicken, a can of motor oil and be on your way without much fuss, sure. But of equal importance: it is all but a given that you will run into an acquaintance or a good friend every time you step into that small town's Walmart. It's a proven fact of life.

Linda pointed out that it was not uncommon for Birch to make the occasional impromptu home visits to the sick and the elderly.

"Bless his heart, this wouldn't be the first time our Birch lost track of time."

It felt good to slow down after the roughhousing with Yolanda. There I was taking blows to the head from that crazed Amazon and then here I was enjoying the company of decent, civilized, everyday folk.

The band started in playing another number. Another Grateful Dead song. No, I'm not a Dead fan. I mean, they're okay. Good jam band. But I lived with a woman once back in the day and she was a Grateful Dead fan, so I heard that band every day for about fourteen months. Some things stay with you.

The rain got down to business then with an abrupt crack of thunder. Not a downpour but that would come any minute now.

The cheerful mood of the small crowd remained undiminished. The band, under shelter of the overhanging tarp, ceased their playing when the deluge commenced. The singer-guitar player in the band announced in a laid-back stoner voice that the party was moving inside. Without being asked, a number of attendees stepped forward to volunteer in transporting the band's equipment into the main building while everyone else went about gathering their belongings to migrate inside.

I encountered Fred, the retired golf enthusiast from yesterday. Ebullient as was his nature, the old duffer held forth with enthusiasm about his favorite band, Pearl Jam. That's right. Pearl Jam. Illustrating, I suppose, two immutable laws, opposite sides of the same coin, you might say: you never can tell about folks, and the book is often more interesting than the cover—at least in the case of *homo sapiens*. People were funneling into the spacious room where yesterday's gathering had been held. I told Fred I was off to find the men's room, to which he directed me before he continued on with the flow of people.

I broke away from the crowd gradually and unobtrusively. I walked over to the door of Birch Sunday's office. I knocked gently, audibly. No answer. I knocked again. I tried the door handle. Locked.

I moved on.

A few of the young men and women residents lingered along the corridors. The scent of marijuana drifted out from behind some of the open doorways. Mostly, the corridors of the main building, lined with doors, were quiet except for those stealing away for a quick high while the band was setting up. When the echoey din of the musicians starting up again could be heard, they too headed in that direction.

To the right of each door, a metal holder set in the wall held a card indicating the occupant's name written in magic marker.

I found Birch Sunday in Janine Richards's room.

Chapter Twenty-One

Birch sat cross-legged on the bed. Head bowed. Loose hair draped over hunched shoulders. Hands clasped before him. The most dejected man in the world. Lost deep within himself.

Think of a college dorm room. Minimal furnishings. That's how the former offices of the mining admin building had been done over to accommodate the live-in residents of Spirit Ranch. Spartan but comfortable. Single bed along one wall. Desk and chair. A pair of discarded sneakers here, an open backpack there. Not cluttered but lived in. Lived in and by a young woman. Wildflowers in a vase next to a CD player. A short stack of CDs by artists with funny haircuts and strange names. Wall posters of a rock bands I didn't recognize. Girl stuff.

"People are wondering where you are, Birch."

"I'll be there." His voice matched his forlorn appearance. "Right now, I need to be alone."

I sat down beside him.

"Too late for that."

He raised his head. His eyes were moist.

"What do you mean?"

"It's time to clear the air. Janine. Where is she?"

"How would I know? She's gone. She's not coming back."

"When did you speak with her last?"

"Why do you ask me that?"

"Because I need to talk with her. I want to know where she is."

His forlorn eyes dropped back to the folded hands.

"I don't know where she is. I haven't seen Janine since her father came for her this morning."

"And how do you and Mr. Richards get along?"

"We've never met."

"Huh. Do you know why he came and got her?"

"Yes. It was on the news. I should be with Janine. Losing her mother. She needs comfort. Reassurance. I understand Janine. I listen to her."

"Are you in love with her?"

"Isn't that obvious?" His answer carried the pain of every country song ever recorded. "She's gone. She's never coming back."

The way he said that made a chill tighten my gut.

"You sound pretty certain about that."

He gave a weak shrug.

"I can feel it. I trust what I feel. Always have. A man like you, McShan . . . do you trust what's in your heart?"

"More often than you might think."

He pondered for a moment.

"The mind is designed to be distracted. Logic can fool us. Emotion is pure. My feelings guide me through my thoughts. And so I *know*. Janine is never coming back."

I said, "Emotions will lead a man astray just like the mind."

"Don't I know it, McShan. Don't I know it."

"If she wasn't involved with you, I've got to ask you, Birch. Was Janine promiscuous while she was here?"

"No."

"Tell me about your feelings for her."

"There's the age difference, of course. Eleven years, though that's not so much when people are old enough to make their own choices. But I have a policy. I never interact at that level with anyone who comes here to celebrate and share our vision."

"I didn't ask about policy," I said. "I asked about feelings."

"My feelings for Janine? Look at me, McShan. Here I sit, wallowing in emotion, mourning her departure. What more would you like to know? Janine is young, yes, but she is not naïve. Strength and vulnerability in one package, that's Janine. She's a survivor. She is a beautiful, caring soul."

The chill in my gut eased. When he spoke like that, it was like he was speaking about Janine's mother.

Marna.

I blinked the thought away.

I said, "If you know where Janine is, then tell me. It's to her benefit to speak with me."

"I told you. I don't know where she is."

"Do you know where Stan Sweetson is?"

He made an unpleasant expression.

"That person! Why in the world should I know where he went?"

"You didn't kill him, did you?"

"Of course I didn't kill him. I've never killed anyone, and I never will."

I said, "I want to think he's alive. I just wonder where Stan took off to. At first, I thought he and Janine were involved. She told me there was nothing to it, but I don't know if I should believe her."

"You can believe her," said Birch. "Stan is gay. I'm the only one around here that he came on to. It's happened before a few times with women but that was a first here at the ranch, me being hit on by another man."

"What happened?"

"I flattered him and thanked him for his interest and promptly turned him down. I have nothing against gays. I've often suspected there could be a touch of bisexuality hidden deeply within each of us. The history of other cultures seems to corroborate the notion. I cast no judgment. I just don't become involved in that way with those who join us here to share our journey."

"Except for Janine."

He sighed softly.

"Janine is attracted to me as a man and me to her as a woman. But I've never touched her in that way. I swear to that by all that is sacred." His voice took on the plaintive quality of a man confessing a mortal sin. "But I yearned to. I cannot lie to you, McShan. Janine would be safe with me. In my arms. In my heart. I would care for her and protect her. Men have always been bad for Janine. I would try to be different."

"Did you know Sweetson drove her to see her mother last night?"

He nodded.

"I saw them drive off together. I didn't know where they were going."

"Do you know a woman named Yolanda? Johnny the Barber's sister."

"I know of her. Why do you ask?"

"Because she paid Sweetson a visit last night."

"I pay no attention to the past entanglements of those who come here. At Spirit Ranch, we manifest our higher selves and seek to break free of the psychic shackles that have held us back."

I thought about that for a moment.

"Birch, what you've got going here isn't really a cult at all, is it?"

His eyes flickered with sudden interest.

"You understand? Yes, exactly. A cult implies religious veneration. Devotion toward a specific figure or object. Rites and ceremonies. That's not what I'm about."

"I see that. There were a hundred people outside who were happy to see their outdoor concert rained out because it brought them a rainbow. The way life knocks the average person around, that's not a bad way to be. I was brought into this because Janine's mother was concerned about the company her daughter had fallen in with. I would have reported to her that everyone I've encountered here at your ranch were good, decent folks from every walk of life."

Birch nodded.

"A place for fellowship. A garden of contemplation in a chaotic world."

The guy was out there but, in a world of snakes like Johnny the Barber and Del Richards, Birch Sunday was trying to make a difference by doing the best he could. He had enough on his plate at the moment without me dumping on him about Del Richards's scheme to grab his land. He would learn about that soon enough.

I said, "This is about more than Janine leaving, isn't it? Tell me, Birch. I really can help you both."

His faraway eyes returned to his clasped hands. He opened his palms. An object dropped from them, onto the bed between us.

I know a pregnancy test kit when I see one. I picked it up. Took a look.

Result: *Positive.*

Birch refolded his hands. He closed his eyes.

He said, "Go away. Leave me alone. I need to meditate."

Chapter Twenty-Two

The sky, dark as twilight, took on a reddish hue. The rain, steady but not abusive. I drove to the *swick-swack* of the wipers.

The death of Marna Richards was less than twenty-four hours old but with the preliminary crime scene reports indicating the cause of death being a blow to the back of the head, it was worth checking in.

I checked in with Rivas. Again, he got right to it.

"Sweetson got in touch. He's at home in Albuquerque. He's flying back here for an interview first thing in the morning."

"That can't hurt. And State is handling it?"

"More or less."

"Sweetson called you because I told him to."

"Yes, he said something to that effect. Thanks for that."

"Always glad to score points. What does he say about last night?"

"He doesn't know a thing about anything. He joined that cult—"

"Rivas, it's not a cult."

"Yeah, I know. But it's what they call it around here so I'm just using shorthand because I'm talking to you."

"Long as you know. I think Birch Sunday is okay."

"I guess he could be. He hasn't broken any laws that we know of."

"So, what does Sweetson say about last night?"

"That he drove Janine to Bisbee to see her mother." It sounded over the phone like Rivas was reading from his notes. "Janine insisted. Made herself a real pain in the ass until he agreed to take her. He even offered to let her borrow the rental car without him having to go but he says the girl told him she was too unhinged to drive. He says he believed her because she was so upset. Obsessing is how he put it."

"Did he go in with her when they got to Bisbee?"

"Uh uh. Sweetson waited out in the car while the girl went in. She was in there for about a half-hour, he says. Sweetson says the girl was stone silent all the way back to the ranch. Wouldn't say a word to him."

"Because she just killed her mother?"

"Maybe. A physical altercation between mother and daughter? Could have happened that way. Whoever gets pinned for it will be facing Second Degree, not First. The victim wasn't clubbed or brutally beaten. We don't have a homicidal maniac on the loose. Someone gave her a shove. She fell wrong and hit her head on the sink. Could be the daughter. Could be premeditated if the prosecutor smells blood. She had Sweetson drive her out and was all wound up on the drive over there. So, maybe she was planning to murder her mom?"

I tried to keep the tiredness out of my voice.

"I'm done playing the Devil's advocate. I'm hoping she didn't do it. Why would she want to? You don't have a motive. I'll tell you what had her so wound up. She'd just discovered that she was pregnant."

Silence.

Then Rivas spoke in a changed voice.

"And how do you know that?"

There seemed no reason at this point to evade, stretch or shade the truth.

"I just came from having a heart to heart with Birch Sunday."

I told him about Birch finding the pregnancy test kit, with its positive result, among the girl's effects. I told him about Birch Sunday being in love with Janine but claiming indirectly that he was not the father of her unborn child.

Rivas said, "I wonder who the father is."

"Working on it," I said. "Soon as I find out, I'll pass it on to you. Uh, did you by any chance get a report on a ruckus down at Johnny's barbershop?"

"No. Should I have?"

"I guess not. Johnny's sister paid Sweetson a visit last night. Not a friendly visit. That's why Sweetson booked out in such a hurry this morning. When you lean on him tomorrow, ask him about Johnny the Barber and Del Richards."

"Why?"

"Why not? It could get interesting."

"It already is. Okay, I'll see about that. Question, McShan. What's in this for you?"

"The truth," I said, and I broke the connection.

Good enough.

Whichever way things cut, the questions Rivas

would throw at Sweetson tomorrow, about his reason for being at The Spirit Ranch, would lead to exposing and undoing Del Richards's land grab scenario.

The cell phone chimed with another call.

I thought about ignoring it and switching off the phone. Things were starting to draw together in my mind. I didn't want to be distracted. I'd checked my calls when I left Gila Springs. No new calls until this one. Agatha had either given up on me or was still allowing me enough rope to hang myself.

I checked the screen. Sherry. I took the call.

She said, "I'm in Tucson. I'm at the airport. I'm on a flight back to LAX. We're waiting for takeoff."

"Do the police know you're skipping out?"

"Yes. They don't care. They have my contact information. They'll let me know if they need me. I'm out of here, McShan. Shaking the dust of Arizona off my boots."

"You're wearing boots? What happened to those stiletto high heels?"

"Smart ass. I'm not giving up my sex appeal, just the bimbo part."

"Well, that's a relief."

A throaty chuckle tickled my ear.

"You had something to do with it. You're quite a guy, guy. A real man. Compared to you, the jerk I've been with took a nosedive. I'm never going back to him. It's over. Del can have everything of mine that I left behind. I'm starting a new life."

"I like the sound of that."

"Hey, McShan."

"What?"

"You want to be part of my new life?"

"Maybe. What have you got in mind?"

"At this point? Just staying in touch. No expectations. But I want you as a friend, if nothing else. Maybe more. I mean, if that's meant to be. So . . . are you my friend?"

"With benefits?"

"A real smart ass," she said. "So how's it going?"

"I'm on the road. I've been thinking over the timeline for last night."

"What about it? Uh oh. McShan, I've got to go. They're telling us to turn off our cell phones. What do you want to know?"

"Last night, could Del have slipped out long enough to kill Marna and drive back again during the time when you were unconscious or asleep?"

"Maybe. It was a rough night. Is that what you think happened?"

"I'm about to find out."

We disconnected together.

I swung the Wrangler off the rain-slick highway, onto the washboard road that would take me to Del Richards's place.

It was still dark as dusk. Lightning had been lancing the sky since I'd left The Spirit Ranch. Finally, the low clouds opened, and the deluge began.

Chapter Twenty-Three

Driving rain slanted down, silver where it caught the light showing from a window at the front of the Richards house. The lightning blazed blue-white, glinting on the sheets of rain. Del's Humvee sat alone in the driveway.

I parked the Jeep Wrangler under the extended branches of a line of mulberry trees that blocked it from sight of the house, or so I hoped. Under ordinary circumstances anyone home would have heard my tires crunching on the gravel road. Not today. Today those sounds were lost beneath the fury of the storm. I'd cut my headlights when I turned off the highway. Unless someone in the house was watching the road, chances were I hadn't been noticed and wasn't about to be noticed. Or so I hoped.

I clipped the Glock 17 9mm's holster to the belt at the small of my back. I left the vehicle, easing the door shut as soundlessly as possible just to be careful. Here at the foot of these mountains where the terrain started to buckle, acoustics could be unpredictable even with this sort of hellacious weather. I sprinted across ten yards of open, sloping ground, heading toward the rear of the house. The rain hammered down, indiscriminate, slapping both me and the hard ground.

I gained an overhang at the rear of the house. I had been doused but I had managed to sprint fast enough to avoid a complete soaking. The only sound in the world from under that overhang was the relentless, thrashing rain. I eased closer to the closed sliding-glass door through which I'd gained entrance yesterday. The heavy rain, splattering the pavement of the patio, splashed me with its mist. The glass door slid open under my touch.

I was indoors.

The same room where I'd first encountered Del and met Sherry. The punching bag in the corner. No lights were on in here, only the faint natural lighting that seeped in despite the storm outside. Rain beat down on the roof like a hyped-up drummer working out an endless solo.

Voices carried to me faintly from somewhere deeper in the house, muted by the noise of the storm. I couldn't make out the words. Couldn't even make out if the voices were male or female. Voices raised in emotion, hardly heard through walls and down a hallway.

Thunder boomed so close the windows rattled and the house shuddered on its foundations.

When I heard a quiet whimpering, I drew up and tried to place its point of origin. This took a few seconds because it was not a human sound. The whimpering came from under a couch against a wall that faced the punching bag.

I walked over and knelt down in front of the couch. In the dim illumination, a pair of glittering eyes peered up at me with fear and hope.

I said, "Hey, Beauregard."

At the sound of his name, the little mutt scooted out from under the couch, tail wagging frantically.

I said, "Frightened by the storm?"

He plopped down on his back in front of me, stubby paws waving in the air. That called for a tummy scratch. The little guy loved it for half a minute or so, forgetting all about the storm. When I took my hand away and straightened to my full height, he didn't waste any time scampering back under the couch.

I was grateful for that. It occurred to me that taking a few seconds to comfort Beau could have resulted in him deciding to stick close. I didn't know what lay ahead but, no question, a lap dog was better off hiding under a couch. Beauregard was smart enough to know that for himself. His intelligent, glittery eyes followed me out of the room, with him wearing that silly doggie grin they get. What a fun game this was. But he stayed right there.

I found myself in a short, carpeted hallway. Glamour shot, head-and-shoulders photo of Janine, adorned one wall. Two closed doors to one side, one open door facing with the corner of a mirror visible. The bathroom.

And a half-open door straight ahead at the end of the hallway.

The angry voices spilled from behind that partly open doorway, still indiscernible thanks to the fury of the storm.

I advanced, my back pressed to the wall. I'd be less

of a target that way if someone with a weapon appeared in the doorway to open fire at me. That's how heated the argument inside was becoming. Given the events of the past twenty-four hours, anything could happen. I thought about drawing my pistol. Having it in hand. No, I wouldn't show hardware. I was the interloper. I was the one trespassing.

The presence of Beauregard meant that Janine was here too. I recognized the voices. Janine and her father were screaming at each other.

I paused just outside the door and gave a listen.

Janine was shouting, "I made Mom promise she wouldn't tell you! God! I was a fool!"

Her words tremored with a raging fury that matched the intensity of the storm.

Her father sneered, "You don't know what you're talking about."

Dismissive scorn.

"Yes, I do! Mom was going to report you to the cops. She told me she was going to be okay, but I should have seen she was in shock after what I told her. She said she never in a million years would have suspected that was going on and I could see it shocked her to her soul. I should have stayed with her. After I left, she stewed and then she called you on the phone and told you off. I thought about it and it's been tearing me apart all day. That's what happened last night, isn't it?"

"Janine—"

"What did you say when she called you? Beg her to hear you out? You drove over to where she was staying and after she let you in . . . *you killed her.* You killed my mother to keep her from telling the world that you raped your daughter."

"You weren't raped."

"I was thirteen, you sick fuck! You messed me up for life!" The venom spewed from her. "You twisted a child's mind and emotions with fear and shame. And you kept on doing it until Boris Temerov rescued me, and after that."

He sneered again.

"That prick got exactly what was coming to him. And so did you. You ended up coming home to daddy, didn't you? So here we are. And here's the score, baby girl. My daughter is fucked up in the head. The court will agree."

"Not after they hear the truth!"

"Ha. You're a screwed up, ungrateful brat. Trying to bring down the loving dad who gave her everything."

The storm outside subsided enough for me to hear Janine say in a low, dangerous voice, "You're a monster. You're the Devil. You ruined me and stole my innocence. Why couldn't you have just loved and protected me like a normal dad so I could grow up to become a normal woman?" Anguish coursed through her every word. *"You killed my mother!"*

Del Richards's voice lowered.

"What happened to your mother last night was an accident. I didn't want for it to happen."

"Bullshit. *Murderer!*"

"Look, I can't undo it. Your mother and I were arguing like we always do. It just got out of hand. I gave her a shove. I didn't mean to do it."

Janine said in a cold voice, "Oh, Daddy dearest, yes, I'm going to bring you down. Damn straight. And I'm doing it right *now!*"

Del Richards cried out.

"*Hey!* What are you doing? *Give me that gun, you stupid slut!*"

At the word "gun", I bolted at the doorway.

The roar of the gunshot was deafening, as if the storm had blown away the roof and was now exploding into the house itself.

Chapter Twenty-Four

An office.

Desk. FAX. Computer. Chair. Couch.

Del Richards toppling to the floor in a wide-armed freefall. Landing on his back between the desk and the couch, his eyes and mouth grotesque, surprised ovals. He did not move. He wouldn't be moving again until someone moved him.

He could have been a guy merely stretched out on the floor, agape at something he'd just discovered on the ceiling, except for the rapidly widening pool of bright red blood spreading from the back of his head, across the tile floor around him.

The scent of burnt cordite hung in the air, and a dissipating haze of gun-smoke.

Janine stood there holding a small caliber pistol down at her side, aimed at the floor. Then she noticed me with eyes that reminded me of a frightened deer. She raised the pistol and aimed it in my direction.

I drew up short just inside the doorway. It occurred to me that maybe after all I should have drawn my pistol before charging in. But then what the hell would I have done? I'd been experiencing pangs of guilt about having to deliver lumps to a crazed biker chick. It wasn't in me to gun down a troubled teenage girl.

I said, "You're not going to shoot me, Janine."

I tried to make it a declarative statement, not a question.

"I won't shoot unless you try to stop me."

"Stop you from what?"

"What do you think? Did you hear what we were fighting about?"

"I heard."

"My mother is dead. My father is dead. My grandparents are dead. I'm carrying my father's child. I won't live in a world like this, and I won't bring my child into a world like this."

I said, "Stop, Janine. It's not too late to turn this around. When I showed up yesterday, you should have trusted and confided in me. So right now is another chance. I can still help you."

"No, you can't. No one can help and what good would it do at this point anyway? I confided in Mom and look what happened. No! It ends here. This way I won't ever have to confide my shame to anybody. Do you think I'd want a single soul in the universe to know what's happened to me? I'd rather die."

"Stop it," I said. "Janine, you're stronger than you think you are. I was starting to get it. The beating he gave that Olympic coach. A lot of fathers might have done the same or wanted to but then there was him isolating you even after the divorce from your own mother. And keeping you isolated. That dark, haunted place deep in your heart. Your mom told me about that. I saw it in your eyes."

Those haunted eyes stared at me. She started to tremble.

I wanted to step forward and put my arms around her. Comfort a soul in torment. I've never fathered any kids, but this girl was the right age to be my daughter. It's hell watching someone in that much pain, especially when they're talking like she was while she held a gun.

She said, "After what he did to poor Boris, flying all the way across the country and practically killing him . . . he told me that what we did . . . that he would never make me . . . do that again. He told me to come home. That . . . that it would never happen again. But it did happen again. He could see I was starting to come unglued. The monster! He told me I should drive out to The Spirit Ranch and meet the people there. I did. I thought he was doing me a favor. That he was . . . over me."

She looked at Del Richards's corpse. She spat on the body.

She said, "Birch Sunday is a good man. Decent. Pure of heart. After I began to know the people at the ranch and how they thought, when I saw how the ideas he shared could change how I looked at life, I started to feel like a spy for my father because that's exactly what I was. And one thing led to another." She indicated the corpse. "This piece of shit changed back again, if he ever really did change. He said he'd come for me again in the night no matter where I was if I didn't do what he told me to do. We had a terrible fight over the phone."

"Sherry told me about that. She overheard part of it but she didn't know what you two were arguing about."

"I knew he was keeping poor Sherry in torment. I wanted to warn her about him but he kept us apart so I could never tell her what he did to me. I did what he said, God forgive me. I could have found a way to contact her but I was so scared of him. It *was* rape, Mr. McShan. It was! Yesterday when Stan Sweetson came at me to blackmail him . . . I couldn't breathe. I can't breathe now. I'm drowning. I can't stand it anymore"

A feral quickness in her eyes.

She raised the gun toward her temple.

Honestly, I could have taken the pistol from her at any point once I entered the room. She was a sweet slip of a kid. A waif in the storm. I had at least seventy pounds on her plus height and build plus I've been trained to take people down without raising a sweat whenever I want or need to. I hadn't wanted it to play out this far. I'd wanted to coax her into making the decision for herself. I've also been trained in talking people out of taking their own lives. Suicide is an initial response more often than you might think when a felony perp is cornered. I'd wanted her to make the decision to live on her own as an empowering first step. But she'd left me no choice.

My left arm straightened to block her right arm from raising the muzzle of the handgun to her temple. My right arm simultaneously snaked around her waist. I gripped the wrist of her gun-hand. I jerked it sharply enough that she cried out. The pistol dropped. A hell of a lot faster than it takes to tell, I used the vise-like grip on her wrist to pivot her toward me as if we were a couple of line dancers and I was holding her with her butt pressed against me.

She didn't struggle. The fight had gone out of her.

The muscular tautness within her relaxed. She became submissive, waiting to see what would happen next. At least, that's what I hoped was going through her mind.

I said, trying under the circumstance to pitch my voice conversationally, "Janine, don't give up. Let me help you, dammit. It's what I was paid to do. It's what your mother wants."

"What my mother wants . . ."

A weak, listless voice.

"Listen to me. Suicides are not permitted on my watch. Are you done acting crazy?"

"Yes, but . . . what are you going to do? What about the police?"

I released her. We both got to our feet.

I said, "The police are the law. I'm justice. How did you get here?"

She indicated the corpse of her father.

"He came and got me from the ranch before I had a chance to see Birch. Poor Birch. He trusted me. I never had a chance to say goodbye."

"I confronted your father at his office," I said. "He knew after that that he had to straighten out things with you one way or another."

She began to say something. Then her irises rolled out of sight and her knees buckled. I caught her before she could drop. She was feather-light in my arms, like a sleeping kid ready to be tucked in. I stretched her out on the couch. She was unconscious. Motionless. Breathing steadily.

The storm outside had diminished to a light shower of rain on the roof.

I considered Del Richards's remains. I considered my options.

Which to do first? Re-imagine? Or call this in? No telling how long the girl would be out and what her state of mind would be when she came around. At the moment she was in no condition to distract or interfere. I would take advantage of that.

I got Rivas on my cell phone.

I said, "Do you know Del Richards's place?"

"I'm a cop. I can find it fast enough. Why?"

"Because I'm there now. Richards is dead."

"Did you do it?"

"That isn't funny."

"It wasn't meant to be."

"Look, Rivas. Flag yourself over here ASAP. No, I didn't kill him. I do, however, have the windup on the Marna Richards kill ready to hand over to you. A feather in your cap."

"I don't wear a cap. All right. I'm on my way. But this has to be by the book, McShan."

"I know that."

"I'll report it. First responders will be there before me. I'm fifteen minutes behind them."

"I'm not going anywhere."

He said, "Good," and broke the connection.

I checked on Janine. Eyes closed. Steady breathing as if in peaceful slumber. Or playing possum. Either way was fine with me. I had to work fast.

The pool of blood was no longer spreading under the dead man's head. His eyes and mouth remained wide open. No sign of an entry wound so it was easy enough to see what happened.

I snagged the pistol from where it had landed on the floor. I used a shirt tail and thoroughly wiped the gun free of any fingerprints. Using my shirt tail to hold the pistol by its barrel, I managed to position the gun in Del Richards's right hand. He was right-handed. Training allowed me to register details like that when encountering primary subjects in an investigation, and I had done that with Richards. His demise was recent enough that his fingers remained limber. Rigor mortis had not yet set in. The body was barely cooling. I knelt beside the corpse to facilitate raising its arm, compressing his finger around the trigger.

I fired a bullet into the ceiling. The gun blast sounded ten times louder than the first because it wasn't in competition with thunder and lightning.

Janine emitted a startled cry. She sat upright on the couch.

"What was that?"

Eyes wide. Back of hand to her mouth. Tremor in her voice.

I said, "You fainted or something."

Her awareness sharpened. She saw me resting Richards's arm at an angle from the body. She saw the wisp of gun-smoke dematerialize, and the pistol where it remained clutched in his hand.

She said, "What's going on?"

"I'm setting this up so your life can keep on going. Tell me what happened."

"He tried to take the gun away from me. We struggled for it. It happened so fast. He was cursing me. He grabbed the gun from my hand and it went off while he was yelling at me. Did you hear what he said? With his dying words, my father called me a stupid slut . . ."

She made a whimpering sound that made me think of the frightened little puppy down the hall.

"Mr. McShan . . . what now—?"

I said, "His mouth was open when he ate the bullet. The angle is consistent with a self-inflicted wound. Here's your story, and we'll both look good."

"Story?"

"Did Birch see you leave the ranch with your father before you came here?"

"I don't think so. I walked alone in a wash that runs behind the ranch. It's a place where I go to meditate. I was trying to think. I saw some of the people setting up for the band concert. They told me Birch was making a house call or something. Then it started raining. No, Birch didn't see me. The poor guy."

Just as I'd held back when talking to Birch, there was no reason at this moment for me to tell Janine about finding the pregnancy test kit she'd left behind. I had to keep this simple for her. One thing at a time.

I said, "Okay, it all fits together. I was there looking for you, but you were either wandering around or had already left. When I saw him, Birch thought you'd already left. So he isn't aware of your activities and whereabouts since the police summoned you and your father this morning. He only knows that I came around a while ago, looking for you. Our story is that I found you."

"All right, but I don't understand."

I said, "He can verify that part of our story. You didn't come here with your father. I don't know what he had in mind but forget that. You came here with me. I hooked up with you a little while ago. We drove here together. I convinced you to confront your father because he admitted to you over the phone that he'd killed your mother."

"He *did* admit that to me just before he died."

"I know. I heard him. We're shifting the time frame but we're not deviating from the truth. Here's what we add on. Your father was tormented by remorse after he killed your mother. He indicated to you over the phone that he was suicidal. We hurried over here to see what we could do to stop him from killing himself. But we didn't make it in time. I'm your witness and you're mine. I'm a licensed investigator on good terms with the sheriff's department."

"Will they believe us?"

"Janine, you'll have to be convincing. I know I can be. I've fixed this to look like a suicide. It's common for gun suicides to fire off a round before shooting themselves. A lot of times that shocks them into not doing it. Sometimes it spurs them on. That's what happened here. Lab tests of his hand will determine that he held and fired the gun he's holding. So how about it? Can you put that over?"

Her gaze lifted from the corpse on the floor. She sat on the couch.

She said, "I'm glad he's dead. If that's a sin, I don't care. He was the most evil man who ever lived. But now . . . Jesus, McShan . . . my family is gone. When Birch Sunday finds out I was there at his ranch to spy for my father, he'll hate me. I'm so fucking alone."

Movement at floor level in the doorway.

Beauregard, his breathing ragged from having run all the way from the back room. Tail wagging. Eyes popped wide with expectation. He held his position on the threshold with the tentative hesitation of a pup wanting to please but not sure of the appropriate behavior.

I snapped my fingers once.

"Come on, boy."

He disregarded me after that and bee-lined straight for Janine, leaping into her lap without waiting to be invited. True to form, he promptly flipped himself over onto his back, ready for a tummy scratch.

I sat beside Janine on the couch. Together we pampered the little guy, Janine reassuring him with soft cooing sounds.

The rain stopped.

Sirens could be heard approaching in the distance.

Chapter Twenty-Five

I t was five months before Sherry and I spent any serious time together.

The week before Christmas we rented a condo at the Tamaron resort north of Durango, Colorado. Our friendship had developed gradually, as long-distance friendships inevitably must. But the foundation for a lasting friendship had been forged that summer in Arizona.

We'd seen each other exactly three times since then. Brief encounters prearranged of necessity in coffee shops at LAX when I was between flights on some assignment or other for Honeycutt Personal Services. For the most part I'd managed to remain in Agatha's good graces since Arizona. Work kept me busy and on the move. Between those airport dates, Sherry and I maintained email and telephone contact and we slowly got to know and really like each other.

That week in Colorado we didn't discuss Arizona until the fourth day. The first days were spent skiing the slopes and with old-fashioned sightseeing excursions to the cliff ruins at Mesa Verde and the 1800's mining town of Silverton.

And, oh yes, we spent most of our alone time in the condo humping our brains out. As can happen when everything clicks just right, the consummation of our attraction delivered in full on the yearning that had been building between us.

Yeah, we were hot stuff.

Sherry was good company.

The world was doing fine that afternoon. We were lounging in the condo, sharing the leather loveseat that faced the fire I'd built against the chill of a snowy day. We were relaxing between an hour in the Jacuzzi and a stroll down to the lodge for happy hour.

I forget now exactly how the subject came up.

Since she was Del's live-in girlfriend, the police had interviewed Sherry at length after his demise. They went on to determine that a combination of the troubled state of their relationship and the fact that Del had murdered his ex-wife contributed to a meltdown of mental stress that resulted in suicide.

Who was I, or Sherry, to dissuade them of that notion?

Anyway, when the subject came up, I said, "They bought the suicide theory like they were supposed to. If Rivas suspected anything, he never said a word. That's where it will stay."

"What about your girlfriend the biker?"

In fact, there were things Sherry knew that the police didn't know, such as my altercation with Yolanda.

I said, "Rivas says Johnny the Barber and his sister

have flown the coop. Left the barbershop and a house they owned and haven't been heard from since."

"Do you think it was their idea to disappear? Or did someone decide to help them along, whether they liked it or not?"

"There's no way to tell. If someone else made it happen, it would be permanent. I'm guessing that's what happened to them."

"You must have some idea about it."

"Sure. Yolanda was responsible for murders down in Mexico that were never reported. That doesn't mean they can't be traced to her by someone wanting to take her out to even a score. They'd take out her brother too. That's the way low level punks like those two usually end up, whether it's Gila Springs, Arizona or New York, New York."

"So who fired the fatal bullet that killed Del Richards? If Janine and her father were struggling over the gun, whose finger was on the trigger when the gun went off? I mean, for real. Did Del shoot himself accidentally or did Janine kill him?"

I'd thought about that, and so I had my answer ready.

"If it had gone to trial, the prosecution would say that she killed him. Janine went there with a gun, so it was premeditated. But here's the deal. Given the end result, who fired the shot is a detail that doesn't concern me in the least. I made a promise over Marna's corpse that the one responsible would pay. Del Richards is dead. That debt has been settled and a promise kept."

Sherry said, "And a young woman has a new chance at life and so does the baby inside of her. Have you heard from Janine lately?"

"Not directly but I've heard about her."

Both of us had initially stayed in touch with the girl via email. Cordial, brief notes from her (full of emojis) letting us know about her counselors and how she was doing. Contact dwindled once her legal affairs were ironed out. So I brought Sherry up to date with the information that had been passed along to me by Rivas in a friendly phone conversation initiated by him over Thanksgiving.

The Sheriff's man reported that he and his wife had spotted Janine in the busy parking lot of the Super Walmart in Sierra Vista. Mrs. Rivas had idly drawn his attention to "the nice young couple" unloading items from their cart into a pickup truck parked one lane over. Janine was noticeably pregnant, said Rivas. She was with Birch Sunday who did the transferring of their shopping items into the bed of the truck while Janine held a scruffy little black dog.

Rivas added some color by mentioning that it had been a blue-sky, mild Arizona winter day. The girl had looked rosy-cheeked and well-fed. Birch Sunday was fawning over her and Janine was visibly basking under his attention.

"She looked well cared for," was how Rivas phrased it.

I repeated that assessment for Sherry, whose response was, "What a boring world it would be if people couldn't change. I've been keeping track of The Spirit Ranch on-line. Membership is increasing every month."

I finished my glass of wine.

I said, "And baby makes three. Janine could do worse."

Sherry said softly, "And so could I."

She shifted slightly beside me on the loveseat and offered up those kissable lips of hers for attention. I accepted the invitation. We commenced kissing.

Serious kissing.

We ended up having a happy hour all by ourselves without ever leaving the condo.

A Look at: Cody's Return
The Justice Trilogy Book One

Return to Chaos!

When Cody's plane touches down at Reagan International, he's a burnt-out case, worn to the bone after a brutal mission into Russia. A runaway high-speed train loaded with stolen nukes and killer commandos came close to ending the life of a man called Suicide—who only accepts missions no one is expected to survive. But all Cody wants now is some well-earned R&R with Sara Durrell, his CIA control officer and lover.

Trouble is, Cody's return finds the nation's capital even more treacherous and deadlier than ever. Two foreign hit teams—one from Dubai, the second with links to the Vatican—are roaming the streets of Washington, dispensing violent death. A beautiful young Arab princess is on the run. Sara Durrell is in the hospital, under armed guard. And the nuke dealer from Russia is also in town, along with the most unlikely adversary Cody has yet to encounter.

Cody's only chance: go vigilante, shake DC to its roots, and hunt down the truth in a city of lies!

"One of the best adventure writers of our time!" —James M. Reasoner, NYT Best-Selling Author

AVAILABLE NOW

About the Author

Stephen Mertz is an American fiction author who is best known for his mainstream thrillers and novels of suspense. His work covers a wide variety of styles from paranormal dark suspense (*Night Wind* and *Devil Creek*) to historical speculative thrillers (*Blood Red Sun*) and hardboiled noir (*Fade to Tomorrow*). Mertz is also a popular lecturer on the craft of writing and has appeared as a guest speaker before writer's groups and at universities.

During high school and college, Steve regularly scandalized his "literary, well-intentioned" creative writing teachers with "thud and blunder melodramas." Throughout military service, travel, and a wide variety of jobs, his goal remained to become a publishing, full-time freelance professional. "It was never a question for me of if, but always when." His first national sale was to a mystery magazine, and his first novel, a detective thriller entitled *Some Die Hard*, was published under the pseudonym of Stephen Brett. Another Brett novel followed, as did a string of mystery and suspense short stories.

Steve's writing output increased dramatically when he emerged as one of the country's most in-demand writers of adventure paperback novels, averaging four books per year for ten years. His work on Don Pendleton's Mack Bolan series is regarded by fans as some of the best in that series. He also created the Mark Stone: MIA Hunter and Cody's Army series, written under the pseudonyms Jack Buchanan and Jim Case respectively.

Stephen Mertz has traveled widely and is a U.S. Army veteran. He presently lives in the American Southwest, and he is always at work on a new book.